BENI'S WAR

Tammar Stein

KAR-BEN
PUBLISHING

KAR-BEN PUBLISHING®
An imprint of Lerner Publishing Group, Inc.
241 First Avenue North
Minneapolis, MN 55401 USA

Website address: www.karben.com

Cover illustration by Carlo Molinari.

Additional images by vadimmmus/Getty Images (tank); Cultura/Charles Gullung/
Getty Images (wall).

Main body text set in Bembo Std Regular.
Typeface provided by Monotype Typography.

Library of Congress Cataloging-in-Publication Data

Names: Stein, Tammar, author.
Title: Beni's war by Tammar Stein.
Description: Minneapolis, MN : Kar-Ben Publishing, [2020] | Includes
    bibliographical references. | Audience: Ages 9–13. | Audience: Grades 7–9.
    | Summary: "Beni is unhappy when his family moves to a remote farming
    community in northern Israel. Everything changes on Yom Kippur when war
    comes, and his soldier brother Motti goes off to fight. As worries mount about
    Motti's safety, Beni realizes that he must act to save the day." —Provided by
    publisher.
Identifiers: LCCN 2019033964 (print) | LCCN 2019033965 (ebook) |
    ISBN 9781541578869 (library binding) | ISBN 9781541578876 (paperback) |
    ISBN 9781541599550 (ebook)
Subjects: LCSH: Israel-Arab War, 1967—Juvenile fiction. | CYAC: Israel-Arab
    War, 1967—Fiction. | Brothers—Fiction. | Jews—Israel—Fiction. | Israel—
    History—1967-1993—Fiction.
Classification: LCC PZ7.S821645 Be 2020 (print) | LCC PZ7.S821645 (ebook)
    | DDC [Fic]—dc23

LC record available at https://lccn.loc.gov/2019033964
LC ebook record available at https://lccn.loc.gov/2019033965

Manufactured in the United States of America
1-46989-47858-3/4/2020

Dear Abba,
I love you. And thank you.

Chapter One

Yoni and Ori are sitting across the aisle from me on the bus. Their heads are close together as they whisper loudly and laugh. I feel that spot between my shoulder blades tingle as they keep glancing at me. We're on the bus for an hour going from school to our moshav. I feel their stares the whole time.

Finally, the bus stops outside our farming community. I hurry off.

Yoni and Ori trot after me. The bus pulls away in a belch of gray fumes. It's just the three of us on the side of the road.

"Hey, loser," Yoni says. "Where do you think you're going?"

Yoni is one of those kids who's twelve but

looks fifteen. He's thickset and half a head taller than me. He's got a shadow of a mustache on his upper lip.

I don't. I'm short and I'm thin and I know that this is going to hurt.

"You're such a little brown-nose," Ori says. Ori is even taller than Yoni, but thin and awkward. His ears stick out, and his nose is small and squished in the middle of his face. He has the longest eyelashes I've ever seen. He reminds me of a giraffe. But a mean one. There's an excited glint in his expression that doesn't bode well for me.

"What do you want?" I ask. I feel my heartbeat shudder in my chest. My palms are sweaty. What a stupid thing for me to say. I know exactly what they want.

"*What do you want?*" Yoni mocks in a high voice. I hope I don't sound that scared. A sharp cramp in my stomach nearly doubles me over.

"I didn't tattle on you," I say. A bloom of sweat prickles across my face. "Why are you acting like this?"

It's exactly the wrong thing to say. A dark red flush spreads over Yoni's cheeks. His hands curl into fists. Ori glances at Yoni and then follows suit, hands clenching at his sides. They both step closer to me.

It takes everything I've got not to back away.

"It's Yom Kippur Eve, and I have to tell my dad that I'm in trouble at school," Yoni hisses. A bit of spit lands on my face. "Everyone hates you. You're the reason the whole class is in trouble."

"You're the one who started it!" I yell.

I don't even see the first blow coming.

His fist catches me right across the face. Pain explodes behind my eyes, and I stagger back, warm blood gushing from my nose and running into my mouth. I gag and spit red.

Ori hesitates—but only for a second. He steps forward and punches me in the gut. My breath whooshes out. For one horrible moment, I can't breathe. I'm bent over, my mouth flapping open and closed like a fish on land. A steady drip of bright red blood from my nose rains down on the black dirt at my feet. Ridiculously, I think of my father crumbling the dirt, calling it good. I'm watering it with my blood.

Just when I think I might never breathe

again, I suddenly manage to suck in a great gulp of warm, dusty air.

I straighten up, trying to stagger away from them, but Ori steps close, shoving me with all his strength. I'm already off balance, so I go flying back. I land on the ground, scraping the heels of my hands and bruising my elbow. Pain shoots up both arms. I scramble back to my feet and lunge at Ori, trying to shove him back. But he skitters away, and I flail at empty air, almost falling again. As soon as I catch my balance, Yoni cocks a fist. I cover my face with my arms, braced for the pain.

But there's nothing. I hear scuffling. I lower my arms, expecting a trick. The first thing I see is Ori's stupid giraffe face slack with surprise.

I shift my gaze to Yoni. For a moment, the sun blinds me. But now I see my brother Motti in his army uniform, his curly hair shining gold in the sunlight like a lion's mane.

He's got Yoni by the back of his shirt, shaking him like he's a naughty puppy. Motti isn't much taller than Yoni, but there's no question who's stronger.

"Two against one, eh?" he says through gritted teeth. "How about we even the odds?"

"You don't understand," gasps Yoni.

"Sure I do," Motti says. He drops Yoni and kicks him on the butt. His black military boot leaves a dusty mark on the back of Yoni's blue shorts.

Ori shakes off his stunned paralysis. He scrambles away. My brother glares at his retreating back. He turns back to Yoni.

"You should be ashamed of yourself. Beating up the new kid. You'll have plenty to talk about with God tonight."

Yoni's face turns splotchy red. His ears are so hot, they're nearly purple. He shoots me a murderous look before he turns and runs to catch up with Ori. But when Ori tries to say something, Yoni shoves him away. They go off in separate directions.

I slowly sit down. I'm sore and banged up, but it could have been worse. My nose has almost stopped bleeding. I wipe away a wet trickle of blood that oozes down.

Motti comes close and squats next to me.

"Beni . . ." I hear the question and the worry in Motti's voice.

I give a half-shrug. Now that they're gone, I start to shake. Hot tears rise up—shame, fear, and relief all mixing together.

"I hate this place," I say, my voice wavering.

"I know." Motti helps me to my feet. Once I'm standing, he takes my face between his hands and looks closely. "Your nose doesn't look broken." He touches the bridge lightly, and I wince. It's tender.

"I know," I say, pulling my face away from his probing hands.

"You'll probably have a black eye. There's no way you can hide this from Ima and Abba."

"I don't care." My voice cracks. "I want to move back."

I see sympathy in Motti's eyes. "It's not going to happen, Beni. They sold the apartment. They're never going back."

His words are like sharp tacks, sending piercing pain in my stomach. I rub it, trying to push away the ache. I miss the white, sun-washed Jerusalem stones, the twisting alleys, my dad's carpentry shop, the smells of baking bread and rosemary, my school, my friends. I miss them all so badly. I even miss grouchy Mrs. Friedburg, who always scolded me for playing too loudly in the courtyard.

"You have to learn to defend yourself," Motti goes on, oblivious to my wandering thoughts. "I won't always be around to protect you."

"I don't need you to protect me," I say. "That's not what this was about. I was fine in Jerusalem."

"Beni," Motti huffs impatiently, "there are jerks and bullies everywhere, even Jerusalem. Remember Dovid? I had to kick his butt after school *twice* before he left you alone."

"That was in fourth grade," I say hotly. "I'm twelve now." My nose throbs in pain. I don't like where this conversation is going.

"Right, that's my point. You have to create your own reputation here; you can't rely on mine."

"You know what, Motti," I say, feeling my temper rise, "just shut up, okay?"

"Beni"—he puts a hand on my shoulder—"you're just too nice. People take advantage of that."

I shake his hand off. "You don't know any-thing about this place. That is not what this was about."

"Okay, so tell me. What happened?"

I try to think of where to start. Motti's been away, first for his basic training, then tanker school. Other than a few weekends, he's not spent any time here at all. He's only home for the holiday. After Yom Kippur, he'll rush back to his tank battalion. He has only the vaguest idea of what I've been going through lately.

The moshav where we live is new. A moshav is like a kibbutz, a little farming town where people work the land, sharing the labor and profits. But unlike a kibbutz, where everyone owns everything together and nothing is owned privately, in a moshav everyone has their own house and plot of land.

My parents love that we live in a house now, not an apartment like we did in Jerusalem. They like the green space, the farm animals in the nearby barns, the orchard with the baby apple trees that will bear fruit in a few years.

I hate those trees. They look like little sticks

with a few sad leaves that shiver in the breeze. The branches and the trunk look too fragile to ever hold up dozens of apples. But my dad loves to go look at them. He often puts his hands in his back pockets and rocks back on his heels, his eyes dreamy.

He'll say, "There's good dirt here." He'll grab a black clod of dirt and crumble it between his wide hands. Then he'll sniff his fingers and smile like he's been smelling fresh-baked bread.

"It's just dirt, Abba," I always say.

"It's a place to put down roots, Beni," he says. And I know he's thinking of my oldest brother, Gideon, who died six years ago.

Our moshav is so small that there aren't enough kids for us to have our own school. Which is why I ride a bus for an hour to get to school at Kibbutz Lavi. There are twenty kids living here, but most are toddlers and babies. I'm one of the oldest.

I hate it.

I had friends in Jerusalem. I had my soccer friends, my chess friends, and even the loud class clowns. My teachers were strict but smart. Now?

There are only two other boys my age in the moshav: Ori and Yoni.

My teacher at my new school is so stupid it hurts. She's clueless. The kids play tricks on her all the time, and she doesn't even realize it. She's an immigrant from France, and her Hebrew is terrible. Which is how this whole mess got started.

Yesterday, Yoni was throwing spitballs into Sara's hair.

I cannot stand Yoni. He always picks on Sara, who lives at another new moshav not far from ours. She wears thick glasses and has a big gap between her teeth. I don't see the big deal about glasses or gap teeth, but she's clearly embarrassed about them. The more she's embarrassed about them, the more kids make fun of her.

"Leave her alone," I said. No one else was going to say it. Not even Sara.

"Why do you care?" Yoni smirked at me. "Is she your girlfriend?"

Sara turned bright red. It made me so mad the way Yoni went on, making everyone's day worse and worse.

I glared at Yoni. "You're such an idiot."

He sneered back at me and said, "*Ata tahat shel hamor!*" Which means *You're a donkey's ass.* A couple of kids near me snickered, and that finally caught our teacher's attention.

She was at her desk at the front of the room, oblivious as always. She always makes a face whenever we call her Morah Yvette. In France, she told us, students called her Madame Monteux. But in Israel, students call teachers by their first name.

"What did you say?" Morah Yvette trilled in her panicky way. She always acts as if she's about to lose control of the class and only screaming at us will help. Something about the way she perched at the edge of her seat, her dumb face looking at Yoni and the rest of the class, got under my skin. Why hadn't she done anything before now?

"He said I'm cool," I said with a straight face. I heard someone swallow a shocked giggle. The rest of the class froze, waiting to see if Yvette would call my bluff. Our teacher knew enough not to believe everything we said. I could see her deciding whether she could trust me or not. I don't know why I lied.

One upside was that I had trapped Yoni neatly. He either had to agree that he'd called me cool or confess that he'd called me a donkey's ass, in which case he would get in trouble.

"It's slang," Yoni said, backing me up. "Everyone's saying it." The teacher looked at the rest of us and, God help us, everyone nodded.

"It's true," Ori said. You could always count on Ori to back up Yoni. "*Tahat shel hamor!* My sister's in the army and they're all saying it."

Yvette's face cleared, and the class continued. Except now everyone kept saying *"Tahat shel hamor!"* in an excited way like it really did mean something awesome. It was actually hilarious to hear all these kids cursing and the teacher just smiling about it.

A few minutes later, Ori passed me a folded note from Yoni.

Nice one.

I looked over at Yoni. He grinned like we were best friends. I felt sick. I didn't want Yoni as my friend. I should never have lied to keep him out of trouble. I didn't smile back. His grin faded. His eyes narrowed. I rolled my eyes and looked away.

The bus ride back to the moshav that day was long and stuffy. We rolled over the green heights of the Golan. I noticed a soaring bird, gliding on air currents. It drifted over the bus and was lost from view.

I imagined Yvette feeling cool with her new slang. I squirmed uncomfortably on the hard plastic seat. I wasn't much better than Yoni picking on Sara.

Then this morning, the principal, Noam, was waiting for us with Yvette.

Apparently, our brilliant teacher went to a staff meeting yesterday. She was excited to try out the cool new slang she'd learned. When Noam brought in a cake that his wife had made for the staff, Yvette spoke up and said she thought he was "*tahat shel hamor.*" She meant it as a glowing compliment. The staff room fell into an uproar. It took a while to sort it all out, but bottom line, our principal figured out we pulled a practical joke on our teacher.

So this morning he yelled at us. "How dare

you mock a hardworking immigrant! How dare you lie to your teacher!"

It went on for a while. And then Sara, trying to help, said it was all Yoni's fault. She must have had to pull all her courage to do that. She'd never spoken out loud in class before. But it didn't help. I really think Noam was planning to make us write an apology letter or something. But once he had someone's name, his mood got even uglier. Yoni is the son of our moshav co-founder, which means he couldn't bear the brunt of all the trouble alone.

Not to worry! Yoni wasn't going down without a fight.

"It's Beni's fault!" he shouted.

And his dumb, obnoxious pet, Ori, hurried to agree. "That's right! He's the one who said it first!"

Everybody was yelling accusations. Sara burst out crying. Noam and Yvette looked a little stunned.

Once they got the class settled, Noam decided the fair thing to do was to punish the whole class, since not a single student had spoken up and told the truth before Yvette embarrassed herself. This made the rest of the class furious at me, since they had almost nothing to do with it. As soon as Yom Kippur is over and we're back in school, all forty of us will be staying late every day for a week washing the blackboards, emptying the trash, scrubbing the toilets, and mopping the floor.

Everyone blames me, the new kid.

And this afternoon, Yoni and Ori kicked my *tahat shel hamor.*

Motti listens to my tale of woe.

"I hate this place," I tell him again, and I've never meant anything more.

I hate everything about it. I hate the smell of cow manure that drifts into our house whenever there's a south-blowing wind. I hate the rooster that crows at four in the morning. I hate the houses that all look exactly the same. I hate the baby apple trees that look so fragile. Too fragile to live. Too weak to put down roots. They will only break my father's heart.

I want to shout, *We shouldn't have come here! We had roots in Jerusalem!* But I choke it back. We'd gone over it before.

My parents refused to listen.

"This all happened because I stuck up for a stupid girl and now everyone hates me and I hate it here!"

"Beni, Beni," my brother says. "You did good."

"What?" I want to shake him. These two days have been a series of mistakes and bad decisions. My face throbs as if to chime in with agreement.

"Yeah. I'm proud of you."

"Then you're out of your mind. I'm an idiot." I touch my nose gingerly. My fingers come away dry. At least the bleeding has stopped.

"Naw, you did the right thing."

I shoot him a "give-me-a-break" look. Just because my nose isn't bleeding anymore doesn't mean I call what happened a good thing.

"I'm serious." He puts a warm hand on the nape of my neck and draws me in close. "Always stick up for people who can't stick up for themselves." His face is close to mine; his pale eyes seem to gleam as they drill into me. "That's what being a man is about. That's what being a decent person is about. And it inspires people to do the same thing. Look what it did for that girl. You made her stronger. That's why she tried to stick up for you. You helped her be brave."

I blink in surprise. I never thought of it that way.

"Maybe it didn't work out exactly like either one of you hoped, but standing up for someone is never a mistake."

I give a half shrug, though I feel a warm glow of pride at his words. "But then I shouldn't have covered for Yoni! Why did I do that?" That's the part that gets me. I hate that guy. Why did I do anything to help him?

"Oh, don't beat yourself up," Motti says, his lips twitching as he tries to hold back a smile. "You couldn't help it. You're so clever. Your mouth was running ahead of your brain. *And* you made him admit you were cool. In front of the whole class! Come on, admit it, that was brilliant and really funny." He grins, and I just burst out laughing. I feel the weight of confusion and anger at myself evaporate.

He ruffles my hair and pulls me in for a hug. He smells like machine oil, soap, and sweat.

I wrap my arms around him, feeling his solid strength. I wonder if he's ever afraid.

We stay like that for a few moments, the sun warming my back. A car passing by slows down and stops. The driver rolls down the window.

"Everything okay?" he asks. I could have used him fifteen minutes ago.

"This is my brother; I missed him," Motti says. I'm thinking the same thing.

"*Nu*, so go home to your mom. What are you waiting for?" says the man and drives off. Everyone in Israel is a former soldier, and everyone knows how much parents worry over their kids in the army. Before the car disappears around the bend, the driver toots his horn and waves to us.

I don't know if it's aftershocks from the fight or from laughing so hard with Motti, but I can't help laughing again. Everything is better now that Motti is here.

"Come on," Motti says, smiling back. "Let's get you cleaned up before Kol Nidre."

We walk to our new house together. I should be thinking up a plausible story to tell my mom about how I got banged and bruised, but instead, I just keep thinking of Motti. My brother is the bravest person I know. He's tough. He's smart.

And I'm the kid who gets a stomachache at the thought of fighting. Fierce as a baby lamb.

All my shame comes flooding back. Motti is defending our country against the people who want to hurt us. I can't even defend myself.

Chapter Two

On Yom Kippur morning, we dress in our white clothes.

It's early, but I'm already sweating. The Golan Heights is wide and open. Then the ground slopes down, and the whole Hula Valley lies below us. The higher elevation means the summers are usually nice, not scorching hot. The winters are bitter and cold; snow is not uncommon. It's a climate perfect for apples and grapes, fruit that doesn't grow in the rest of Israel. Until six years ago, it belonged to our enemy, Syria. They used the Heights to fire mortar and artillery rounds down on towns and farms in the Hula Valley. After the Six-Day War, the Golan Heights belonged to us.

You never know about the weather in October; it could be chilly or hot. This year, it's hot. Unusually hot. There's a *hamsin*, a wave of hot wind that's pouring out of the desert in the east and baking the air around us. So much for a cooler climate.

Our moshav is pretty secular, but it doesn't matter how religious a Jew you are—on Yom Kippur it feels like the whole world stops in its tracks to pray and think about how to be better in the upcoming year. This year, Yom Kippur falls on Shabbat, so it's a double holy day.

Then again, maybe not *everyone* feels that way. Because at eleven in the morning, we hear the sound of an approaching vehicle. It's so abnormal that everyone comes out of the synagogue to see what's going on.

A military jeep speeds into the moshav.

"We're declaring an emergency," says the soldier from the open-top jeep. "Everyone must evacuate." He's a young guy, not much older than Motti, in a loose-fitting army uniform. He's tanned and dusty.

"What?" someone says. "Why?"

"The Syrians," he says.

Everyone kind of gulps. The Syrian border is only five kilometers from here. Less than a ten-minute drive. Instantly, I feel the space between my shoulder blades start to itch, like someone's staring at me.

"There's going to be a bus coming around noon. It'll bring you to Kibbutz Lavi. They're preparing emergency shelters."

"You've declared emergencies before, and nothing happened," Yoni's dad, Baruch, says. "This is Yom Kippur; this is Shabbat. I'm not violating God's law for a hunch." Yoni's dad has a heavy belly. He's standing so close to the jeep that his belly pushes against it, looming over the soldier in the driver's seat.

"The IDF thinks the Syrians are coming," the soldier says. He narrows his eyes at Baruch. Everyone's listening. "You think you know better? Stay. But if I were you, at the very least I'd put the women and children on that bus."

"What for?" Yoni's dad blusters, his face growing red. People are watching the heated conversation like it's a sports match. "The past three times we went on alert, nothing happened. This is the holiest day of the year!"

"The Syrians are coming," the soldier says. "I hear they don't care that much about the Jewish holidays."

Baruch's face twists in anger. I can see the resemblance between father and son. I half-wonder if Yoni's dad is going to start punching the soldier.

"We don't need some kid telling us how to—"

"Look," the soldier interrupts him, "you do what you want. The bus is coming. No one's making you get on." He turns the key in his jeep and the engine rumbles back to life, spewing gas fumes. It's like a slap to hear that sound on Yom Kippur. "But you are taking your life and the lives of your family into your own hands."

He zooms away, leaving a plume of dust behind him.

"We're not doing it." Yoni's dad turns to the crowd. His eyes are stabbing in their accusation. "What's the point of being Jews in Israel if we run like mice? My dad in the shtetl used to hide under the bed when a pogrom started. We are not running."

"We're not mice if we leave when the Israeli military tells us to evacuate," my mom says. My dad puts his arm around her in support. I catch them exchanging a look and a subtle nod.

A few people, mostly women, murmur in agreement. Motti and I exchange looks. The adults start debating whether to board the bus when it arrives.

"I'm going to pack," Motti tells me quietly. "I'll ask the bus to drop me off on the way to Kibbutz Lavi." There's a major intersection called Ginosar on the way. He could get off there and find a ride to Tel Aviv, then catch a bus to his base in the south. Soldiers don't have to pay for bus tickets, and it's easy to hitchhike when you're in uniform.

"But you only got here yesterday," I protest. "You have another week of leave."

"Something big's happening. My leave is going to be canceled for sure. The military would never send a bus on Yom Kippur if it wasn't serious."

In the end, that seems to be what the adults

24

decide as well. Ori's dad—a thin, slight man with a wispy goatee—makes an announcement: "When the bus arrives at noon, we will all board. Please go home and pack a small bag. Only the necessities for the next twenty-four hours. We are still obeying God's laws—no one should break their fast, and please pack only what is absolutely necessary for your health."

Baruch's mouth twists and his nostrils flare. I make sure to stay out of his way. Yoni doesn't. He tries to ask his dad something. In a flash, his dad's got him by the ear. He gives Yoni a little shake. "I don't have time for your stupid nonsense," he says. By the time he lets go, Yoni's ear is bright red, his face bone white.

Yoni catches my stare. His mouth twists and his nose flares with the same furious, hateful look as his father. Yoni's brother, Dor, a little three-year-old, tugs on Yoni's shirt, wanting something. Yoni shoves him away so hard that Dor loses his balance and tumbles over, scraping his knee on the gravel. He starts crying loudly.

Yoni looks horrified at what he's done but seems frozen in place.

I walk over and crouch by the little boy. "Hey buddy," I say. "You're okay."

Dor looks at me, his brown eyes big and shimmering with tears. He shows me the pink scrape on his knee and shoves two plump, dirty fingers in his mouth.

"Want to see *my* scrape?" I ask and show him the crusty scab on my elbow. It's much bigger than his.

His eyes widen in admiration.

"Want a piggyback ride?" I ask.

His fingers still in his mouth, he nods.

Our upstairs neighbors in Jerusalem had twin boys. I know my way around toddlers. Nothing cheers them up like a piggyback ride. I heft him on my back. He's solid and heavier than he looks. As we sway up, he wraps his arms around my neck, his fingers soggy from his mouth.

I must make a face because I hear a noise. It sounds like a laugh, but when I look up, Yoni won't meet my gaze.

I turn my back on him and gallop like a horse, making Dor laugh all the way to his house.

At noon, we all stand at the small turn-in on the side of the road where buses stop. It's not a proper bus stop; there's no bench or overhang. Just a lamp post, currently turned off. The sun beats down on us; there's no shade anywhere. I scuff over the rusty brown spots where my nose bled into the dusty dirt the day before. The adults are all still fasting, and, judging from the miserable looks, they're all thirsty and wishing they were in their cool, shady homes.

Time ticks by slowly. 12:15. 12:30. No bus.

The younger kids whine and fret in the heat. I sit on a rock, bored, annoyed, and uncomfortable.

"Maybe this is a good thing," my mom suggests. She has the gift of always finding the bright side. "Maybe they called off the evacuation."

12:45 . . . 1:00 p.m. Not a single vehicle passes us. It's Yom Kippur, and everyone else in Israel is busy praying. It's hard not to feel a little foolish. The entire moshav waiting on the side of the road. What are we doing here?

"What a waste of time," Yoni's dad mutters. "This is what we sacrificed Yom Kippur for? Waiting on a bus that doesn't show."

As much as I don't care for Baruch, he has a point. What if in the end they don't send a bus or even bother to tell us the evacuation's been canceled?

The sky is a brilliant blue. The flat land around us is yellow with dried grasses, dotted with short scrubby green bushes. Occasionally a breeze drifts by. It cools the sweat beading on my face, neck, and back. It's a sleepy kind of day. There's no feeling of danger. It's hard to believe anything could be wrong. I scan the hills, looking for—I don't know what. Syrians? Military vehicles? Regardless, there's nothing out of the ordinary. It's just an October day. As if agreeing with my thoughts, a buttery yellow butterfly flits by.

Finally, at 1:30, a bus rumbles around the curve in the road. The bus driver, an older man with a heavy mustache and thick sideburns, parks the bus and opens the door. He doesn't seem particularly anxious about the fact that he's running an hour and a half late.

As people surge forward, he holds out his hands. "Relax. Take it easy. There's plenty of room for everyone."

We take his advice to heart. Dulled from an hour and a half in the heat, tired and thirsty, everyone moves slowly. One by one, families start to board, juggling babies, toddlers, and bags. Some of them make little nests of blankets for young ones to lie down and nap during the long ride ahead.

The bus is three-quarters filled when Yoni's mom, Ronit, suddenly realizes she forgot the baby's pacifier. Shoshi is crying incessantly.

"It's not a necessity!" Baruch thunders.

"It is," Ronit says, her voice rising over the screams of the baby in her lap. "She won't stop crying without it." Our neighbor Miriam, who also has a baby, nods emphatically in support of Ronit.

"You've got time," the driver quickly assures them. He clearly doesn't want to drive for an hour with that howling. "I won't leave until two. You're the last moshav to evacuate."

"Yoni, go get Shoshi's binki," his mom says.

Silently, Yoni slips off the bus and hurries toward their cottage.

Motti sighs in irritation. Another delay, and he's clearly anxious to get to his base. He makes his way to the driver, and I see the two of them talking about the day's events.

It's 1:45.

Motti looks back at me. "Beni, I—" But I never get to hear what he has to say.

Because that's when the mortar shells start to explode all around us.

Chapter Three

The explosion rocks the bus. I feel the vibrations in my bones.

"Off the bus!" the driver shouts. "Everyone off! Run to shelter!"

There's a terrible scramble as people leap out of their seats, hurrying down the narrow aisle, tripping over blankets and bags to get out the door. My parents and I are sitting near the back. Moms and toddlers in front of us stumble over each other as babies and little kids scream in terror. It feels like we will never make it off the bus.

Motti told me that in the military he learned to identify the kind of artillery by the sound of its shriek. He even mimicked the sounds.

There's a cough sort of sound when a shell exits a cannon. Then, as the shell travels through the air, it makes a shrieking noise. It sounds like a mosquito, if the mosquito were the size of a dog and coming in at a thousand meters per second.

I don't know what kind of artillery the Syrians are firing on us, but the air is filled with coughs—*fweet fweet fweet*—and then with high-pitched shrieks again and again. Then *BOOM! BOOM!* Shell after shell lands, closer and closer to our moshav as Syrian artillery units get their bearings and fix their aim. Each *BOOM!* is louder than the last. It shakes the ground beneath us, kicking up clods of soil, filling the air with smoke and dirt. My eyeballs vibrate inside my head. Outside the bus window I see people sprinting here and there in confusion.

"Run to our house, Beni!" my dad shouts in my ear. "As soon as you get off the bus, just run."

I nod. Each cottage in the moshav has a small family-sized bomb shelter.

My mom is mumbling something under her breath. It sounds like prayers but I can't quite catch what she's saying.

Finally, after tripping and stumbling our way down the aisle, we make it to the front of the bus and down the front stairs. My dad has his arm around my mom. He's looking for Motti, who disembarked ahead of us. There's an explosion and the sound of glass shattering. The windows blow out of the cottage next to us, scattering broken glass.

"Go, Beni!" my dad yells. "Straight to the house!"

Our house is normally a five-minute stroll from the bus stop. It suddenly seems as far away as Antarctica. The ground shakes under me, urging me on.

I'm sprinting when I bump into someone. Yoni's mom is struggling with Dor and the baby. Yoni hasn't had time to return with the pacifier, and his dad is nowhere around. The baby is shrieking, and Dor has wrapped his arms around his mom's leg. She can barely walk, and Dor won't listen as she screams at him to let go.

Without thinking about it, I snatch up Dor, plucking him off his mother's leg. He grips me in terror, almost choking me. Trying to catch my breath, I stumble. Dor's weight throws off my balance. A screaming shadow passes nearly overhead. Instinctively, I duck, and that's the final tipping point. I lose my balance and fall flat on top of Dor. He's tiny under me, and I don't have time to brace myself. All my weight lands on his little body.

I scramble off him. He has a stunned look on his face. He's not crying, which is bad, but I hope I only knocked the wind out of him. I scoop him up in my arms and race to my family's shelter.

My feet pound under me. Dor's weight slows me down. My house seems impossibly far away. My breath saws in and out of my chest. I've lost sight of my parents and Motti. I only hope they're ahead of me now, already safe inside our shelter. Our house is one of the farthest in the moshav, and soon there's no one outside but me and the limp boy in my arms.

Every second stretches out like eternity. It feels like I have always been running. Like I will always be running. Like I will never ever be safe again.

But finally I see my house.

The metal door of the shelter is open, though it should be closed. My parents' worried faces peer out, looking for me. They made it in before me.

"Run! Run! Hurry!" my mom screams, waving me toward them.

Another shell hits, exploding nearby, showering me with dirt.

With a final burst of speed, I plunge down the stairs into the cool, welcoming safety of our shelter. The heavy door closes behind me with a clang. I collapse on the concrete floor, twisting as I fall so that Dor is on top of me this time.

For a few moments, I literally cannot move. My limbs sprawl heavy and limp, twitching occasionally. I lie in the cool safety, stunned that we survived. The barrage of explosions outside doesn't stop.

"Where were you?" my dad yells. "What took you so long?"

It takes my eyes a moment to adjust to the dim light in the shelter. Gradually I'm able to make out the cot on the floor, the shelf with emergency rations—canned juice and chocolate bars—and the radio that lets us communicate with other shelters. My parents have knelt next to me. The relief of being safe inside is so huge, I can't seem to move.

"Dear God, Beni, are you hurt?" my mom asks, patting my arms and legs. When I don't answer right away, her voice climbs higher. "What's wrong? Tell me!"

I open my mouth to speak but even my vocal cords are paralyzed. My mouth is dry. I open and shut my mouth helplessly. Finally, I stop trying to speak and just shake my head no.

My dad tips a canteen of water into my mouth and I swallow gratefully.

"I'm fine. Where's Motti?" I croak out. "Is he okay?"

"He probably went to a different shelter," my dad answers, reaching for the radio. "I'll call around."

"Who do you have there?" my mom asks, noticing the limp child in my lap for the first time. "Is that Dor?" she says.

I swallow another sip of water, finally able to speak properly. "Yes."

"Is he okay?" she asks, her voice rising with concern. She gently lifts the small boy off me.

Dor hasn't cried or spoken since we entered the shelter.

I sit up. "I don't know," I say, my voice cracking.

"Was he hit? Is he bleeding?" My mom touches the boy all over, looking for injuries even as she asks the questions. "Dor," she coos. "Dor, baby. It's okay. We've got you. Does something hurt?"

"I fell on him," I say, my stomach turning in fear and guilt. "When we were running. I fell right on top of him."

Another explosion booms close by. I instinctively duck.

"It's okay," my dad says. "We're safe. You did the right thing bringing Dor here." He hugs me, crushing me into his barrel chest. "That was brave of you."

My mom, meanwhile, hasn't stopped her examination of Dor. As she runs her hands along the back of his head, he winces and gives a little whimper.

"Oh, you have a big lump there," my mom says, still in a high, sing-song voice. "You got a big bump, huh? I bet it hurts."

His bottom lip curls out as his chin starts to quiver.

"Oh, baby," she says, gathering him up in her arms. "That was scary. I know."

Dor tucks his head into my mom's chest and pops his thumb in his mouth. He's not screaming, which I'm grateful for. But he looks pale, which is worrying.

While my mom is busy with Dor, my dad asks on the radio if anyone has Motti, and the Perlmutters respond that he's with them, safe. My dad also talks to Ronit, Dor's mom, to let her know we have the toddler.

"He's sleeping right now," he says. He doesn't mention the bump on Dor's head. There's no point in making her frantic with worry when there's nothing she can do for Dor until the shelling ends. Radio communications need to be short to keep the waves available for other communications. Plus, there is always a chance the Syrians are listening in.

Now there's nothing to do but sit and wait for the barrage to be over.

"It won't take long," my dad assures us. "It's just the Syrians wishing us a meaningful Yom Kippur. Everyone's prayers will really come from the heart this year, am I right?" He waits for us to laugh at his joke. My mom and I manage to smile. "It's going to stop any minute now."

But the shelling goes on. Hour after hour.

Dor falls asleep on my mom's chest. She carefully lays him down on a blanket spread on the cot. He doesn't stir even at the loudest booms.

After a couple of hours, my mom shakes him awake, but he's lethargic and hard to rouse.

"Dor-leh," she croons, stroking his sweaty hair. "Wake up, sweetie. Have some juice."

He moans, his eyes fluttering, but doesn't wake.

"I don't like this," my mom says. "This isn't normal toddler behavior."

"Let him sleep," my dad says. "He's had a bad shock. Sleep is the best thing for him."

I can tell my mom is uneasy, but there's not much we can do for Dor right now. Every so often, I glance over at the toddler, but he remains asleep, curled on his side like a little seashell. I replay that moment when I tripped. I wish over and over again I could have twisted to the side so that I didn't land on him.

The radio in our shelter can connect us to the other shelters, but we don't have a transistor radio that will get us news. My dad keeps insisting this is a localized shelling. This is what the army was trying to warn us about. It's our bad luck the Syrians are firing so many shells into our moshav, but it's not a sign of anything more serious.

Our moshav has been shelled before. A few mortar rounds landed in our fields a few months ago. We waited it out in the shelter, and within an hour, it was safe to be outside again.

"They'll stop soon," my dad promises.

But hour after hour passes, and the explosions outside continue. Where is the Israeli army? Where is the air force? Why isn't anyone stopping the Syrians from firing on us?

My father's reassurances slow and finally stop. We can catch whiffs of smoke and of rubber burning, the smells drifting into our shelter from outside. Our moshav is being obliterated.

Chapter Four

It's after five by the time the barrage of explosions finally stops. We wait until someone from the army calls us on our radio and says that it's safe to come out.

When we emerge from our shelter, we're braced for the worst. Will our little town be nothing but rubble and dirt?

My dad walks out first, followed by my mom carrying Dor. I bring up the rear, my heart beating unpleasantly fast.

The smoke and dust hit me as soon as I step outside. The choking smell of burning rubber is much sharper outside. One of the cottages nearby has had part of its roof blown off. An electricity pole has fallen down, and there are live wires shooting sparks. The burning-rubber scent comes from a nearby car that's been on fire for hours. The metal skeleton is blackened and naked, shimmering in the flames. There are craters and divots in our yard, and my mother's flowers have been blown to smithereens.

"Oh, look!" my mom gasps. We follow her gaze out to the fields. There are so many fires burning among the crops that it looks like Lag Ba'Omer, a festival of bonfires. All the work, the hours in the hot sun, the new crops ready for harvest—for nothing.

One by one, our neighbors emerge from their shelters.

"Ruti!" "Avi!" "Yehuda!" They call to each other, everyone grateful that the others are okay. We slowly take inventory. Who's here? Who's heard from whom? We need to organize quickly. The military radio operator was clear: Get out of here and fast.

No one's going to argue with him on that.

Two people have sprained their ankles, tripping as they scrambled for cover. One young child fell down the stairs into the shelter and is badly bruised. But that seems to be the worst of it, other than the fact that Dor is still sleeping, more than three hours later.

"We've lived here for three years, and I've never seen anything like this," Ori's dad tells mine. "Hundreds of shells fell."

I keep scanning, squinting through the smoke. "Motti!" I cry as soon as I spot my brother. I run over, leaping over the twisted path between us. The once-smooth concrete is now jagged and torn.

He opens his arms and crushes me in a quick, hard hug.

"You okay?" he asks, cupping my face.

"I've never prayed so hard on Yom Kippur," I say. My heart lifts to see him crack a big smile.

"You and me both," he says and ruffles my hair. "But we're all fine. That's what matters. No one in the moshav was badly hurt. Isn't that amazing?"

"Come quickly!" someone cries out. "A miracle!"

We rush over. The bus, parked on the side of the road, is completely untouched.

The driver, who's emerged from one of the shelters, quickly inspects the bus and turns the ignition. It fires right up, the engine rumbling reassuringly.

A few people clap and cheer.

"All right," the driver says, hitching his pants. "This time we board quickly and go. There's no way to know how long it's going to stay quiet."

He doesn't need to tell us twice. Everyone jostles into a line, babies in arms, toddlers in tow. Anyone who's not carrying their own baby is pressed into service to help with someone else's kid.

My mom has handed Dor to Ronit. I see them murmuring, heads bent over Dor's groggy body.

A minute later Ronit passes me as she climbs aboard the bus. She's too busy with Dor to look at me. He lies limply in his mother's arms, his little mouth open and a pearly drop of drool hanging off his lip.

All the other toddlers are crying or whining or clinging to their mothers. I know there's something wrong with him. Something that I caused when I fell on him. My stomach twists and cramps. Why didn't I try harder not to fall on him? Why wasn't I more careful when I ran? I wish someone else had seen him and helped instead of me. Anyone else would have done a better job.

We pack onto the bus, and Motti perches on a seat near the driver again, urgently giving him instructions. I know my brother. He wants to rejoin his military unit as fast as he can.

As soon as we're all seated and the bus heads out, the driver turns on the news.

Technically, it's still Yom Kippur. There shouldn't be anything but static on the radio. But no one is surprised when the familiar voice of the news announcer comes on. We catch him in the middle of a string of nonsense code words. *Bat cave. Silver rock. Night owls.* It's called a silent mobilization. All sorts of prearranged signals that only the soldiers of those specific units would recognize. "*This is not a drill,*" the announcer says. "*Please report immediately to your deployment station.*"

Finally, he finishes the unit call-ups and proceeds to the heart of the matter.

"*And now, a news update,*" he says in his smooth, serious voice. "*This afternoon, in a coordinated surprise attack, Syria and Egypt crossed our borders and, in doing so, declared war on the State of Israel. Our forces are meeting them on the field of battle on our northern and southern borders.*"

War! There's a shocked murmur on the bus before people hush to hear the rest of the news.

After hours of shelling, we knew something bad was happening. But it's a blow to discover the situation is even worse than we thought. Syria's border begins less than five kilometers from our moshav. If Syrian forces have already crossed into Israel, that means they're close, awfully close. And Egypt is the large, powerful country to our south. There was supposed to be an unbreakable, well-defended line along the Suez Canal between us and them. Yet apparently, they've already crossed it and are in our territory. It's unthinkable.

The announcer ends his update, and the broadcast switches to creepy piano music. My parents are sitting on the bench in front of me.

"What is that awful music?" I ask.

"Beethoven's Moonlight Sonata," my mom says, almost in a daze. "It's very famous. Must be someone's idea of calming music." I find it melancholy. It sounds like something you would play at a funeral.

Around us, the bus erupts in agitated chatter.

"War!"

"Two fronts!"

"A surprise attack on Yom Kippur!"

"We'll teach them a lesson they'll never forget!"

"It took six days to beat them last time," Yoni's dad growls. "It will take even less this time around. Mark my words, we'll be in Damascus in three days."

"Yeah, I hear the hummus is pretty good in Cairo," someone from the back of the bus calls out. "And Syrian falafel is even better. What do you say we go find out?"

Damascus is the capital of Syria, and Cairo is the capital of Egypt. The Egyptians and the Syrians are probably saying the same thing about hummus and falafel in Jerusalem, our capital.

But I don't care about hummus in any capital.

I'm thinking about Motti. Motti going off to war. Gideon, my oldest brother, went to war in '67. He didn't come back.

As if he can feel my worry, Motti looks back from his seat behind the bus driver. Our eyes meet over the heads of the rest of the moshav members arguing and making predictions. The younger kids fret and cry, unnerved by the commotion on the bus. In the midst of all the chaos, Motti winks at me. He motions me to come sit with him.

"This will all be over by Sukkot," Ori's dad says from his seat across the aisle. Sukkot is in four days.

A few people add their agreement. Even though we've been caught by surprise, every-one seems confident that this will be another short war.

I make my way up the aisle, rocking as the bus takes a turn on the road and hits a pothole. Motti grabs me as I trip over a bag in the aisle. I drop onto the seat next to him.

"The driver's going to stop at Nafah to let off some of the guys who are based there," Motti tells me.

Nafah is the military headquarters in the Golan. Most of the younger dads at the moshav belong to the units that defend the Golan.

"Is that where you're going to get off too?" I ask, even though Motti belongs to a unit that defends the south.

"No, I asked the driver to stop at Ginosar since we pass right by it on the way to Kibbutz Lavi," my brother says. "I need to get to my unit, and the Nafah guys aren't going to want to spare any vehicles to take me south."

I nod silently.

We sit side by side as the bus rolls on. Night is falling. The Golan is thinly populated, so there are no street lights, no city lights to keep the dark at bay. The few lights that do exist were turned off because of a mandatory blackout. The temperature rapidly drops, so even though the day was hot, it's cold now. I didn't grab a jacket when we left the moshav, and I shiver as a tendril of cold air slithers down my neck. Several military transport vehicles pass us, hurtling toward the battlefront. People on the bus cheer as they fly by.

Motti and I don't cheer.

After a moment, I rest my head on Motti's shoulder. He is solid and warm. He puts his arm around me to keep me from rocking too much on the bumpy ride. I could stay like this forever. I wish the bus would keep driving, on and on, driving all through the night, driving all day, driving until Sukkot in four days, when the war might be over. But all too soon, the bus slows down. We've arrived at Nafah.

The base is full of activity. There are jeeps and command cars coming and going. Buses arrive with reserve troops who have been called up. Trucks pull out, loaded down with fuel, shells, and spare parts for the soldiers holding the line against Syria. Ambulances are already running to and from the front, and there's a helicopter coming in for a landing. Six men, younger dads from the moshav, hop off the bus. Their wives and children wave and wave, pressed to the window as the men pass through the front gates and disappear into the chaos of the base. Our driver doesn't waste a second. As soon as the men are off, he reverses and drives away, eager to get off the Golan.

We're getting closer to the Ginosar intersection, where my brother will leave us.

I wrap my arms around Motti and squeeze, burying my face in his chest. I can feel his heart beating solidly under my cheek. He presses his lips to the top my head.

I am shaking. I'm cold, hungry, tired, and scared. It's too much. I feel helpless and useless, totally overwhelmed by the situation.

"Be strong, Beni," he says. "Everything's going to be okay."

"Sure it is," I say. "But just in case, can I have that in writing?"

"You'll see," he says, giving me a squeeze. "Everyone is doing their share, doing their best. And that's enough."

The bus slows down. We're at the intersection.

"Is this good?" the driver calls to Motti.

"Perfect," my brother says.

He stands up and I feel a sudden chill where his warmth used to be. He grabs the small pack he prepared before we were shelled, and after quick hugs with my mom and dad, he disembarks off the bus. My dad is too old to serve in the army. He watches with a pained, worried look as Motti stands at the curb, eyes scanning for cars heading south. He puts his arm out, his thumb raised. He has a long night ahead of him. A ride to Tveria. A bus to Tel Aviv. Another bus from there to the northern edge of the Negev. All said and done, he'll probably arrive at his base around dawn. There, he'll join his unit and head farther south, to fight the Egyptians in our newest war.

My parents share a sad, tired look. They've done this before. My dad fought in the Independence War in 1948 and the Sinai Campaign in 1956. Gideon fought in the Six-Day War in 1967. And now, Motti is off to war on Yom Kippur, 1973. My mom rests her head on my dad's shoulder, and he wraps his arms around her, holding her close.

The bus doesn't linger. As soon as Motti is off, the driver pulls away from the curb, heading for Kibbutz Lavi.

I crane my neck, looking out the window until Motti disappears from sight.

Chapter Five

Kibbutz Lavi has been expecting us since noon. When we finally pull in at seven in the evening, they welcome us with open arms.

Their dining hall is set, the food ready for the adults to break their fast and for the kids to dig in. Lavi is a traditional kibbutz where the children all sleep together in the children's house instead of with their parents. To make room for us, the children have moved to their parents' cabins for the night, and all their beds have been remade with clean sheets and blankets for us.

Since most families from our moshav left without clothes or diapers for their little ones, the kibbutz has organized a quick drive. There are piles of clothes for families to choose from. There's another pile of clean diapers. A small side table is set with bottles of formula warming in bowls of hot water.

One of the kibbutz residents is a doctor, and I watch as Yoni's mom hurries over to him, carrying Dor in her arms. I start to walk over, wanting to hear what the doctor has to say, when suddenly someone grabs me with a glad cry and envelops me in a bear hug.

It takes me a moment to realize it's my teacher, Yvette.

"*Mon pauvre petit*," she babbles in French. "*Tout va bien?*"

"What?" I say. "What?"

"*Pardon*," she says. "It's hard to speak in Hebrew when I'm so upset! When your bus did not arrive, I was fearing the worst! There's war! *Mon Dieu*. I never thought such a terrible thing could happen."

She gazes at me again and then pulls me in for another hug. I hear her sniffle back tears of happy relief.

"You're not mad at me?" I ask slowly.

She says something in rapid French. I blink.

"Yes, I was upset. But how can I still be angry?"

Some of the strain and knots in my back release. I've been feeling so guilty. My shoulders drop at her words of forgiveness.

"I'm really sorry," I say. "I shouldn't have tricked you. I don't know why I did it."

She takes my hands in hers and gives them a warm squeeze. "Because you are twelve and sometimes your mouth shares your funny thoughts before you can think it through. And because you wanted to look smart and tough in front of your new classmates. It's hard to be new," she says simply. "I know how it is."

I never thought about the fact that we're both new here.

"When did you move to Israel?" I ask.

"One year ago," she says. "My family is still upset with me. They want me to come home. Even before this situation, they worried so much that I was not safe here. And now they will be beside themselves with worry for me. I haven't been able to speak with them. I cannot get an open line to make an international call from the kibbutz."

"Why did you move to Israel?" I can't imagine moving away from my family.

"I thought it would be a grand adventure. I wanted to live in the Jewish homeland and never be worried about being Jewish. When I was growing up in France, the children in my school would call me a dirty Jew. I was the only Jew in my class. Sometimes they would say I stole from them, and the teacher would always believe them. I had this dream that I would move to Israel and that I would finally find my true home. But I've been lonely. Israelis are like sandpaper. You are so rough."

"We're Sabras," I say. "Prickly pears. Hard and spiky on the outside, but sweet and mushy on the inside." I can't imagine living somewhere where I was the only Jewish kid in school.

"It's true," she admits. "I've met some people who are warm and kind. But still . . . I am full of splinters from their tough outsides."

Suddenly she sees Yoni and Ori walking by. With another cry of happiness, she rushes over to them. They look as astonished as I must have looked a minute ago. She clutches both of them to her. I never realized how much she cares about her students. I wonder if it's because we're the only people she has to care about here.

I decide to tell my mom about her. She'll take the teacher under her wing and introduce her to some nice people she can be friends with.

I wander over to the buffet set up with food. As I take a plate and start helping myself to chopped cucumber and tomato salad, Sara steps up next to me.

Our eyes meet, and we both smile in relief.

"We've been so worried for everyone from your moshav," she says.

"You guys weren't shelled?" I asked.

"I don't know what happened with our moshav, but we evacuated in the morning. Everything was quiet then."

"Oh."

"As soon as the bus driver dropped us off, he turned right around to get you. When he didn't come back, we started to get really worried. What happened?"

I fill her in on my afternoon, but I don't say anything about Dor. I feel too awful to talk about it. I try to look for him and his mom, but I can't find them in the crowded dining hall. I spot my parents in a knot of adults, heads bent together as they discuss the latest news.

Sara and I eat our dinner together.

Her brother, Yuval, is a tanker with the Seventh Armored Brigade. His unit was famous for their bravery in the Six-Day War. Their motto is "exposed in the turret" because even though it's safer for the whole crew to be inside a tank with the turret hatch closed, the tank commanders ride standing up with the hatch open, exposed to enemy fire and shrapnel, so they can see the field better and fight more effectively. Yuval was already with his unit at their base during Yom Kippur, so she doesn't know where he is now.

Sara and I chat idly, neither one of us wanting to talk about what our brothers are going to deal with in the next few days.

After our dinner, I find my parents and hug them goodnight. The adults are going to stay up in the dining hall, drinking coffee and listening to the news, though there's nothing new being reported. A lot of rumors are swirling, but no one knows anything for sure.

It's clear that our stay here will be temporary, though. The kibbutz can't host this many guests for long. Tomorrow, people will be going off in different directions, wherever they have relatives who can take them in for the next few days. The kitchen staff are laying out a tower of sandwiches for the moshav families to take with us on our long rides tomorrow.

Sara and I walk to the children's house and pick bunk beds. We're going to sleep in our clothes.

At ten o'clock, the kibbutz staff announces that they plan to turn off the lights. We're supposed to go to sleep. Everyone expects a long day tomorrow.

Once I'm in the bunk, I can't fall asleep. Everyone around me tosses and turns, and the large room with its rows of bunk beds seems to hum with unquiet energy. I think about my friends in Jerusalem. My neighbors from our old building. My teachers. I hope everyone is okay. I try not to think about Motti.

There's a prayer that we say on Yom Kippur: *On Rosh Hashanah it is written and on Yom Kippur it is sealed—how many shall pass away and how many shall be born, who will live and who will die, who in good time and who by an untimely death . . .*

Basically, on Yom Kippur, God decides who stays in the Book of Life this year . . . and who doesn't.

I stare up at the bottom of the bunk above me, unable to sleep. My thoughts keep circling: Who's in and who's out of the Book of Life?

Chapter Six

The next morning, Sara and I stand at the gate of Kibbutz Lavi watching the khaki-colored military vehicles driving past. It's a long army convoy, and all the traffic is going in one direction. North toward the border with Syria. North toward our moshav. North toward war.

Every single person in those vehicles is facing danger to protect us.

"I wish I could do something," I say. There's this strange twisting feeling inside me. I'm sad and proud and lonely at the same time. "It doesn't feel right just to watch them go."

Sara doesn't answer right away. She's gazing at the convoy, face tight with concern.

"Like what?" she finally says. She sounds

tired and out of sorts. No one slept well last night. "We're not soldiers, yet. We're not trained for this."

I think of falling on Dor. She's right. I'm not qualified to help people in this situation. I kick at one of the black basalt rocks that litter the high plains of the Golan. We were raised on the stories of the brave kibbutzniks who pulled together, who worked during the day and fought during the night. Some of the greatest Israeli heroes, like Hannah Szenes and Moshe Dayan, were first kibbutzniks, who risked all to protect their fellow Jews and their country.

Hannah Szenes parachuted into enemy territory, paying the ultimate price. Moshe Dayan was fourteen years old when he joined the Haganah and seventeen when he lost his eye in combat.

While I don't want to die, and I don't want to be maimed, I can't help yearning to make a difference.

"Do you think they packed lunch?" Sara asks, interrupting my gloomy thoughts. "Maybe they were in such a hurry to load up and head out, they didn't remember to take food. We could hand them some food as they pass by. That would help, right?"

I blink in surprise. On the one hand, who forgets food? But on the other hand, what if she's right and each soldier was only thinking about their own gear and their own job? It could happen. And they'll be in the field for hours. Maybe even days. Food can't hurt.

"That's a great idea," I say, feeling a rising excitement.

She smiles hesitantly. "You think so?"

"Yeah. Let's go ask the kitchen staff if we can take some of their sandwiches."

Sara and I run to the kitchen, and the staff quickly get behind our plan. We set up a small assembly line, wrapping cheese-and-cucumber sandwiches in wax paper and stuffing them into paper bags. Each bag also gets an apple and a slice of honey cake from the Yom Kippur Break-the-Fast meal.

Pretty soon, we have two dozen of these lunch sacks. Sara and I pile them into an empty milk crate and hurry back to the front gate.

The convoy line is still going strong. But

before we can cross the road and approach any vehicles, a loud rumbling sound stops us.

A line of tanks is driving up on the left side of the road, the one that's usually used by traffic going in the other direction.

It's not that I'm surprised to see tanks. Of course, we need tanks at the front. But they're driving on the road instead of being loaded on flatbed transporters. Motti explained to me once that tanks shouldn't drive on paved roads because their treads—the very thing that makes them unstoppable in sand or loose dirt—rip the asphalt to bits.

But here they are, a line of five heavy armored tanks, their long sand-colored turrets facing forward, coming toward us. The commander of each tank stands looking out of the open hatch, exposed in the turret.

It's scary to see tanks approaching. I know they're on our side. But they're massive and deadly-looking, their bulky metal frames like the bulging muscles on some mythical beast.

And Motti is right—the massive tank treads leave deep, jagged-toothed grooves in the road, cracking and pulverizing the gray asphalt. They are literally breaking the road they are driving on.

For a moment, my heart squeezes in cold dread. We live in a notoriously frugal country. We're careful not to waste water, electricity, or food. I cannot imagine any military commander allowing his tanks to rip up a perfectly good road. Unless whatever is happening on the front is so bad that damaging a good road is the least of our worries.

As I'm digesting all these thoughts, Sara lets out a joyous cry and runs toward one of the tanks.

"What are you doing?" I yell at her, but she's waving wildly, jumping up and down on the side of the road. The soldier riding on the front tank says something into the headset in his helmet and raises his fist up in the air. His tanks and the tanks behind him all slow down and come to a stop.

I can finally make out what she's saying.

"Yuval! Yuval!" Sara shouts. "Hello!"

I trot after her, holding the crate full of food.

"Sara-leh!" the soldier calls out. "Shalom!"

Sara stops next to the heavy, looming tank. Her head doesn't clear the top of the treads. Yuval hoists himself out of the turret and quickly clambers over the side until he's standing on the armored skirt that covers the treads.

He squats down and when Sara reaches out, he easily lifts her onto the metal skirt next to him. He takes off his helmet, and brother and sister embrace. When they separate, I have to keep myself from laughing.

Yuval might look tough in his olive-green uniform and black lace-up boots, but he also looks just like his sister. He has the same gap between his teeth, the same thick glasses, the same dark curly hair. I don't need anyone to tell me they're related. Especially now, side by side, their faces are almost identical.

"Who's this?" Yuval asks Sara, catching my look.

"This is Beni, my friend from school."

"Oh!" he says. He gives me a friendly, assessing look. His brown eyes are magnified behind the thick lenses of his heavy black eyeglasses. "Sure, I've heard all about you."

Both Sara and I turn bright red.

"Yuval," she says, punching him in the arm.

He laughs, his white teeth shining against his tanned skin. "Okay, sorry," he says. He drops a kiss on her head. "It's such a treat to see you, sweetie, but I've got to go."

"I know," she says. She looks down at her scuffed brown shoes and then buries her face in his chest. Her arms wrap around him, and she squeezes so hard that he gasps.

"Whoa there," he half-laughs as he pats her head. "I can barely breathe."

"Be careful, okay?" she says, muffled into his uniform.

"Absolutely," he says with easy confidence. "We've got this."

Reluctantly, Sara lets go. He lowers her back to the ground.

"We'll see you in a few days." He pulls on his helmet.

"Wait," I say, before he can climb back up. "Do you want food to take with you?" I hold up the crate in my hands to show him the bags.

"Food? Fantastic!" he says, smiling and

flashing the gap in his teeth. "We always need food! Guys," he says into his headset, "my sister and her boyfriend brought us food! There's enough for all the tanks."

We hear faint cheers coming from the open hatch. Sara's face is now the color of a tomato. I feel my face heat up as well.

"He's not my—" she stutters. "I can't believe you just—"

I carefully avoid making eye contact with Sara. I just hand up the crate and Yuval grabs four bags. He winks at me, looking very pleased with himself at the trouble he's caused.

I hurry to the tank behind him, and the commander there shimmies out and grabs some food bags from the crate, looking delighted. I do that for each tank and at each one, the soldiers shout thanks from inside the tank. Sara's idea to give them food was really brilliant.

Once my crate is empty and every tank has its bags, Sara and I step away from the road. Yuval gives the command, and the line of tanks moves forward, their tread links clinking and grinding, and their engines belching diesel fumes.

Sara and I wave wildly as these hulking machines of war get smaller and smaller. Their pale yellow sides, painted to blend in with the desert, glow against the darker landscape of the Golan.

"That was amazing!" I tell Sara. "Your brother is so cool."

Sara grins. "He's pretty great," she says. "But you know, I never told him you were my boyfriend . . ." She's turned bright red again, barely able to get the words out.

"Brothers," I say, and roll my eyes.

She looks at her feet for a moment before sliding a look at me. We share a smile.

It's a beautiful autumn day. The sky is a crisp blue, and the sun feels like a warm, friendly pat on the back. Though it was weird to see the tanks drive by us, I do feel better about our odds on the battlefield. It's hard to imagine anything capable of stopping them.

"Beni!"

I turn to see my mom hurrying toward me. "What are you doing here? We've been looking all over for you. We found a van to take us to Saba and Safta's. Who's this?" she asks, noticing Sara.

"This is my friend Sara, from school," I tell her. "We just saw her brother drive by on a tank!"

My mom smiles at Sara in an automatic greeting but is instantly distracted by the news that tanks just drove by. She takes in the state of the road, and her mouth forms an "O" of surprise. "This is going to make the ride interesting."

We all gaze at the road for a moment. A migrating stork passes over us, gliding on some invisible air current. Its shadow dances over the broken chunks of asphalt before floating over the orchard on the other side of the road.

"Sara"—my mom turns to her, visibly pushing away the worry and dismay—"it's nice to meet you. You must be so proud of your brother."

Sara nods, shy as always with a new person.

"Do you know where you're going from here?" my mom asks, making conversation. She's good at not letting other people's embarrassment make her feel awkward. She just keeps asking friendly questions. No one can resist her for long.

"My parents said we're going to Safed," Sara says. "My aunt and uncle live there."

"We are too," my mom says. She gives Sara a side hug. "I bet we're riding together. Let's get back and get organized. They want to leave soon."

Sara looks toward the horizon where her brother disappeared. After a second, she sighs and turns away. My mom gives her shoulder a squeeze.

"Be strong," she says softly. "We'll get through this."

Sara gives her a questioning look. My mom smiles reassuringly. She doesn't have her makeup on this morning. We didn't bring anything with us when we left the house. Her eyes look smaller than usual. Tired. Her lips are pale, washed out without lipstick. I never see her without makeup, and it's disorienting how different she looks. Older. More fragile, somehow.

"Beni's brother Motti is also a tanker. He's with the southern command. He's heading south to Egypt." Even if my mom's face looks different, her voice is the same, steady and confident.

"Beni told me," Sara says softly.

"So you know that we have the best tanks and the best soldiers. They'll be fine."

My mom has invested a lot of brisk confidence in her words. I can tell they cheer Sara. My mom has a strong force to her personality. She can take charge of a room just by walking in. But I know her, and to me, it sounds like she's trying to convince herself as much as Sara.

I look back over my shoulder, though the tanks are long gone. The broken road looks like the wake of a boat, foamy and churned.

I spare a thought for our house back at the moshav. What's going to happen to all our things? We didn't even lock the door on our way out.

The van taking people to Safed is parked in the small lot by the dining hall. My parents, Sara and her parents, plus a couple of other families are milling nearby, waiting to board. We're ready because we have nothing to pack. I spot Yoni, but not the rest of his family.

It reminds me that I haven't seen them since we arrived last night.

"Have you seen Dor this morning?" I ask my mom. "How is he doing?"

"Dor and his parents left for the hospital last night," my mom says, her voice deliberately casual. "They took little Shoshi with them, but I told them we'll take Yoni until they can come get him."

My stomach drops at the news.

"Dor will be fine," she assures me. "It's better to be safe than sorry with the little ones. And kids bounce back quickly from these things." She pats my shoulder. "Don't worry about him, sweetie."

"Yoni is coming with us to Safed?" Sara asks with dismay, catching only that part of my mom's explanation. She doesn't know about Dor, of course, or that I'm the reason he's hurt. She catches my eye and makes a face.

But while Sara is annoyed that we'll be spending so much time with her nemesis, my heart sinks for a totally different reason.

Little Dor is in the hospital.

Because of me.

Chapter Seven

Sara and I sit next to each other in the van and watch the hilly, rocky landscape slide by the window. Between December and April, the hills and plateaus of the Golan are bright with wildflowers and grasses. But now, after the hot summer, everything is parched and yellow. Dead.

Millions of years ago, this was volcanic land. Large black rocks—pitted with tiny empty pockets, where hot, bubbling gases escaped—litter the ground like building blocks tossed by a toddler.

Yoni sits up front by the driver. Other than nodding hello, he hasn't said anything to me. I can't think what to say to him. Sorry for hurting your little brother? Sorry for sending him to the hospital? Sorry for trying to do something good but ending up doing something disastrous?

The first part of our trip is on the broken road. The driver goes slowly, and we sway and bump over the dips and bends of the cracked pavement. But soon we turn west, toward the middle of the country, and leave the ruined road behind. It's a hilly landscape, and other than the occasional military vehicle, there's no one on the road but us. Large eucalyptus trees, planted more than forty years ago by settlers looking to dry out the swamp land, sway their long droopy branches in the slight breeze.

We pass through the Golani Junction, past a memorial to the fallen members of the Golani infantry, a famous army brigade that has fought— and lost soldiers—in every Israeli war. During the Six-Day War, fifty-nine Golani soldiers were killed fighting the Syrians. You can't go far in Israel without passing the scars and memories of past battles, past bloodshed. It's normally easy for me to ignore, but not today. There is someone alive right now whose name is going to belong on that memorial by the end of the war.

The radio in the van is tuned to Galatz, the military station. It plays upbeat songs by the Beach Boys, Elvis Presley, and Arik Einstein, and it gives news updates every fifteen minutes. But the updates don't say much, recycling the same facts that we've heard all day: We have been attacked. We are fighting back.

By this time six years ago, our air force had destroyed the air forces of Egypt, Jordan, and Syria with minimal losses to us. There's nothing like that on the news today. Of course, six years ago we were ready for war. And as of yesterday, most of the country was in synagogue, praying and fasting.

We ride along the long, circular road that climbs the hill to get to the center of Safed. The driver lets us off at the old Ottoman-built fortress that's now a local school. It's at the top of the hill, in the historic center of the town. Safed is thousands of years old, mentioned in the Talmud, written about by Roman chroniclers, conquered by Christians during the Crusades, by Muslims in the thirteenth century, by Turks during the height of the Ottoman Empire.

I can't help but think how strange it is that this patch of land has been fought over for so long, like a bone tugged between a pack of wolves for thousands of years.

Safta and Saba, my dad's parents, are waiting for us at their house, a short walk from the school, down white cobbled lanes. Before Sara and her parents head to her uncle's house, we make plans to meet in the school courtyard in the morning.

Yoni comes along with my parents and me. We walk side by side on the narrow, worn sidewalk. I keep sliding glances over at him, but he walks with his hands shoved in his pockets and his head down, watching his feet.

I never told my parents that my bruises and bloody nose were courtesy of Yoni and his best friend, Ori. They know we aren't close, but they have no idea that we fought. My mom probably thinks she's doing me a favor, giving us a chance to get to know each other. But it's not going to work. Yoni and I are never going to be friends.

When we arrive at my grandparents' house, they welcome us in with open arms, fussing over us, offering freshly baked cake, candy, and soda.

"Oh, Rivka," my mom says. "You shouldn't have."

"I didn't buy too much," my grandmother says, a bit defensively. "I just needed to make sure we'd have enough eggs and milk for the week. You know how quickly they'll run out of those."

Since the men who drive the produce trucks tend to be young, most of them deploy to the military during national emergencies. Which means that during mobilizations, like now, there aren't enough drivers to drive the eggs and milk to the grocery stores. My grandmother is right. It wouldn't be fair to panic-buy and hoard more than your share, but the first people at the store are the ones who will have eggs and milk this week.

My grandparents didn't know that Yoni was coming, but they quickly adjust the sleeping arrangements. My parents still get their usual room, but Yoni gets the small loft where I usually sleep, and I get the couch. I force a smile and nod.

"Of course," I say. "No problem."

But I'm not happy. I love that little loft. There's a narrow window up there that has the best view in the whole house, overlooking the Galilee and the ridge of hills that turn blue and purple in the evening. Motti and I used to sleep up there together, like two sardines, head to feet, because neither one of us wanted to sleep on the old musty couch that smells like cigarette smoke. But I'm not about to sleep like a sardine with Yoni. So he'll have the loft to himself and I'll make do with the smoky couch.

We gorge ourselves on all the goodies that my grandparents set out while we fill them in on what happened to us at the moshav. Yoni stays mostly silent, which my mom takes as worry for his brother and homesickness for his parents.

She puts an arm around him and gives him a squeeze. I want to tell her, *Don't bother. He's a jerk.* I expect him to push her away. I watch him with narrowed eyes, ready to jump to my mom's defense the minute he's rude to her. But instead, to my shock, Yoni closes his eyes at my mom's touch and leans against her shoulder, turning to her for comfort. He's taller than she is. She pulls him into her for a giant, warm hug.

They stay like that for several moments, Yoni and my mom. His face is tucked into the crook of her neck, so I can't see his expression. After a while, she pats his back and ends the hug. Yoni steps back. I stare at him, trying to catch his eye, but Yoni carefully keeps his face turned away from me.

* * *

That night, the second of the war, I sit on my grandparents' nubby orange couch and watch a program on their television. We don't own a TV, so this is a treat. There's a movie on: *The Emperor's New Clothes*. My grandparents say it's not the regularly scheduled show. Much of the country is under a blackout curfew. The television programmers know that everyone is home with their kids, and they need to do something to keep them entertained.

My parents and grandparents are glued to the small radio in the kitchen.

Yoni has excused himself and climbed up to the loft, saying he wanted to sleep. I know he isn't going to sleep at eight in the evening. Besides, he has a clear view of the television from up there. At one point, I turn my head and see him lying at the edge of the loft, chin in hand, watching the screen.

When the movie's over, I walk into the kitchen, catching the end of the hourly update. The announcer tells us that Israeli tankers and artillery are meeting the Egyptians in the south. To the north, the fighting against Syria in the Golan Heights is going well. We haven't heard anything from Motti, of course, but it's too soon for anything he's written to reach us. My dad warns us not to expect a postcard for at least a week. Plus, he might not think to send it to Safed, so it could take even longer to get here.

Golda Meir, our prime minister, reads an announcement. "We have no doubt that we shall be victorious," she says firmly. But other than reassuring us that our army is doing its job, she gives no specifics. It's clear that this time, we really were caught off guard.

Golda is famous for once saying, "We Jews have a secret weapon in our struggle with the Arabs. We have no place to go." That phrase echoes in my mind. Even here in Safed, deep into Israel's territory, we're fewer than fifty kilometers from the Syrian border. Where would we go if their forces breached our defenses?

My dad clicks off the news. With a deep sigh, he walks out of the kitchen and into the living room. I follow him out. He opens the drawer in the narrow end table and rummages around, pushing aside old bills, ticket stubs, and scribbled notes until he finds a pack of cigarettes. It's my grandmother's "emergency" pack.

My dad hasn't smoked in years. But my grandparents occasionally smoke, and with the nerves and worry, he clearly can't resist the temptation. He tears open the cellophane and wiggles out a cigarette. He finds a book of matches from a fancy restaurant in town. The match flares orange, and he bends toward it as he lights his cigarette, the flame coloring his face. He looks tired. When he blows out the match, the woody, sweet smell of smoke fills the room.

"Really?" my mom asks, leaning against the doorframe from the kitchen, wrinkling her nose and waving the air in front of her.

"One won't hurt him," my grandmother says. She walks past my mom and joins my dad on the couch. "Let him have a moment of peace."

The two women exchange sour looks. They always battle over my dad. My grandmother wants to spoil him, and my mom wants him to make healthy choices.

My dad shakes his head. I look from my dad to my mom to my grandmother to my grandfather—who's staying silent—as if I'm watching a soccer match.

My mom presses her lips in annoyance, but when she sees he isn't grinding out the cigarette, she turns and walks back into the kitchen. My dad stays on the couch, staring straight ahead and methodically sucking the cigarette, blowing out streams of smoke through his nose like a dragon.

Shrugging, my grandmother reaches for the pack. My dad slides it to her, and soon she's lit a cigarette as well. My grandfather doesn't say anything, but he doesn't join in either.

"Abba," I finally say, breaking the heavy silence in the room, "we're going to win, right?"

"God willing," he says, almost absently.

"So why are you smoking?" I persist. "You're just making Ima mad at you."

"I'm thinking."

"Smoking helps you think?"

"Beni," my dad says wearily, "would you see if your mom needs help in the kitchen? It'll make her happy." He turns his cigarette around and stares at the glowing, smoldering end as if there's something written there.

I blink in surprise. But my dad stays that way, so finally I go into the kitchen.

I find my mom busy scrubbing the counter. I remember seeing my grandmother wipe the counters after dinner, so I'm not sure why my mom thinks they need cleaning again. It isn't even her kitchen.

"Can I help?" I ask awkwardly.

She looks up with surprise but smiles warmly. "My Beni-boy," she says, pressing a kiss to my forehead. "Here." She hands me a rag that smells like bleach. "Wipe down the stove."

We work in the kitchen for nearly an hour, taking plates and glasses out of the cabinets, wiping down the shelves with lemon juice and vinegar, and re-shelving the dishes. When we finish, the kitchen smells like salad dressing, and as far as I can tell, everything looks about the same. But my mom seems happier, so my dad was right about that.

By the time we walk back into the living room, my dad has opened the window and set up a fan to clear out the smoke. Cool night air fills the room with its special mountain smell. My parents exchange one of those looks: frustration, sadness, and worry. They must be thinking about Gideon and Motti. I glance back and forth between them, trying to read the message. My dad rises from the couch and slips an arm around my mom's waist. She leans her head on his shoulder.

"Goodnight, Beni," she says, looking back at me. "Sweet dreams."

My grandmother, watching them, grinds

out her half-smoked cigarette in the nearly full ashtray.

My parents go to their room and shut the door. I hear the low murmur of their voices but can't make out the words. Safta and I spread a sheet over the couch where I'll sleep tonight. She turns out all the lights and presses a kiss that smells of smoke and tobacco to my forehead.

In the unfamiliar room, dark shadows form shapes and crevices where none should exist. I can hear the ticking from the hall clock.

My parents' worry fills me with a hollow fear. What did they hear in that broadcast that I missed? Is it only that they know Motti is fighting somewhere out there in the Sinai? Casualties are inevitable—we all know that. But Motti is in a tank. Even if the war isn't over by the time he gets to the front, he'll be surrounded by bulletproof metal.

"You promised me," I whisper, picturing Motti in his uniform, somewhere in the desert. "Stay safe."

I can hear rustling from the loft. Yoni's awake. I forgot about him.

"Beni," he says. "Are you talking to me?"

"No." I feel my face flood with heat. I roll to my side, tucking the blanket around me.

"Oh."

We're both quiet for a while. The hall clock's ticking fills the room.

"The thing with Morah Yvette," he suddenly says. "I'm not mad about that anymore."

I was expecting him to say something about Dor. "Okay."

"I just wanted you to know that."

"Okay," I say again. I want to say so many other things, but I can't. I want to ask about Dor and if he's mad about that. I want to ask if his dad always treats him like that. I want to ask if he thinks we'll have a moshav to return to when this war is over. But I don't. Maybe I'm scared of what his answers would be.

"Goodnight, Yoni," I finally say.

"Goodnight, Beni," he answers.

It takes a while, but eventually I fall asleep.

Chapter Eight

The next day Yoni joins me to meet Sara in the courtyard by the old fortress. I don't want him to tag along, but I can't exactly leave him with my parents and grandparents all day. There would be too many uncomfortable questions about why I'm not taking him with me. We leave the adults sitting tensely around the kitchen table, listening to the news. My grandmother pointedly cleans the stove, re-wiping everything my mom and I cleaned last night.

As soon as Sara notices Yoni, her shoulders hitch up. She turns slightly away from him, making it clear that she wishes he weren't here.

Yoni has his hands shoved deep in his pockets, shoulders up around his ears, nearly identical to Sara. I feel a small pang of guilt. We're all stuck together because I hurt Dor. It's my fault.

"What should we do?" I ask, kicking a small pebble. It bounces off the pale stone wall of the fortress. I stress the word *we*.

Yoni shrugs, not meeting our gaze.

"Want to go to my uncle's auto shop?" Sara offers. "He said we could come by."

"Let's go," I say with extra enthusiasm, so we don't stand awkwardly any longer.

As we follow Sara along the narrow, pale cobbled lanes, I think again of how ancient this city is. Safed is famous for its long history of Jewish mystics. Even when most of the Jewish people lived in the Diaspora—first Babylon, then Rome and Spain, eastern Europe and the Middle East—there were Jews living in Safed. Legend has it that when holy men no longer study Torah in Safed, the Jewish people will perish.

Sara leads us past signs hanging above arched entries that lead to courtyards, private homes, and apartments. Some of the gates are decorated with mosaics of pomegranates, sheaves of wheat, fat globes of purple grapes. It's a visual reminder that this is the biblical land of milk and honey. I'm no holy man, but I have studied Torah at school. I know it well enough to know that this is also the land of sword and bloodshed.

We follow Sara out of the old city, with its tight alleys and crooked trees, and into a newer section. The road is wider; the buildings are square and plain. We pass several beige apartment buildings before arriving at her uncle's shop. Two cars sit outside. Inside, one car is up on a lift, and another is parked next to it. The smells of machine oil and diesel gas greet us.

"Hi, Uncle Mickey," Sara says. "I've brought my friends."

A little yippy dog hurries over, barking hysterically but keeping a safe distance from us. I look for the dog's owner, Mickey. I spot a pair of shoes and stained overalls sticking out from under the car that's not on the lift. It's what the Wicked Witch from *The Wizard of Oz* would look like if a car fell on her instead of a house. Fortunately, unlike the witch, Mickey's not dead. At the sound of Sara's voice, the legs slide out, and there's a man lying on a wooden pallet with wheels. It's a clever way to be able to slide in and out from under a car.

"Hi, Sara's friends," he says, grinning and displaying that family trademark of a big gap between his front teeth. The yippy dog races from us to Mickey and back toward us again.

I can't help but grin back.

"Easy, Goliath," Mickey croons to the dog. "They're not here to hurt anyone."

"Goliath?" I choke. The dog could be mistaken for a fluffy rat. It has large, bugged-out eyes, floppy long-haired ears, and a suspicious expression on its face.

Goliath rushes at Yoni, barking and growling, his yips of dislike growing more and more frenzied. Clearly he's a good judge of character.

Sara crouches down and makes little kissing sounds. With a last growl at Yoni, Goliath hurries over to her. She scratches him under his chin. He gives a happy groan and flops over on his back, letting her rub his stomach.

"What an ugly dog," Yoni mutters under his breath. He's got that familiar sneer on his face.

"Are these the friends you brought to work?" Mickey asks her, rising to his feet. He hasn't heard Yoni's grumbles. "I lost my assistant to the military call-up. I could use some help."

"Really?" I say in surprise.

"What? You got something better to do?"

"But we don't know anything about cars."

"You think I can't teach you some basic car repair?" Mickey asks. "You don't give me enough credit."

"Anyway, speak for yourself," Sara says, rising to her feet. "I've been helping my uncle since I was six."

"Boys," he says, rubbing grease-stained hands with delight, "it's your lucky day. Today you become men."

Yoni's face goes slack in surprise.

"My bar mitzvah's not for another six months," I say jokingly.

"Bar mitzvahs are all well and good," Mickey says, with a twinkle in his eye. "But I say, until you can change an oil filter, you're still a child."

Yoni mumbles something under his breath. It's not a compliment. He's probably still in a bad mood from being the only one Goliath hated on sight. I say that's one smart dog.

Mickey finds us dirty overalls to put over our clothes. Then we step over to the car and get to work, learning the art of changing an oil filter. Sara goes with her uncle, sliding under the car on another wheeled pallet. Apparently, she's already a grownup in her uncle's eyes.

Mickey shows us the oil pan and the drain plug that keeps it sealed.

Goliath patters around, giving me a sniff. He tries to do the same with Yoni, but Yoni pushes him away with his leg. It's not quite a kick, but it's forceful enough that Goliath jumps back and gives a little "grrrr" from the back of his throat.

Mickey peers up from under the hood, giving us a sharp look. "I accidentally bumped him," Yoni says. "He got underfoot."

Mickey looks at him suspiciously, but Yoni has perfected the straight-faced lie.

"Well," Mickey says flatly, "be more careful."

As soon as he turns back to the car, Yoni shoots him an evil glare.

Giving Yoni a huffy sniff and a sneeze, Goliath trots over to an old couch cushion on the floor. He stamps around in a circle and settles down on it, chin on his paws, keeping a careful eye on us.

"Remember," Mickey says, holding a wrench. "To the right means tight, to the left is loose." He fits the wrench on the bolt and tugs to the left. When the bolt won't budge, he picks up a rubber mallet from his lineup of tools and taps at the wrench to help with the torque. The bolt gives way, and black sludgy oil starts gurgling out. Mickey has a pan to catch the old oil. He doesn't spill a drop.

He shows us how to examine the gasket on the plug. We'll need to check it for wear and tear and replace anything that looks loose or nicked. This one is fine. Once the stream of oil slows to a trickle, Mickey replaces the plug, using the wrench and tapping it gently to the right with the rubber mallet to seal it.

He lowers the car and pops open the hood. He takes out the old, grimy black oil filter and puts in a clean one. Then he unscrews the cap for the oil pan, fits in a funnel, and pours in four bottles of clear yellowish oil. He lets the hood down with a clang.

"And that's how it's done," he says. "Got it?"

Being a man doesn't look that hard.

Yoni and I step under the next car on the lift. Just an hour ago, I would have looked at the mess of pipes and tubes and machine parts in utter confusion. Now I can clearly identify the oil pan. Yoni hands me a wrench, and together we pry off the bolt that holds it on. I'm ready for a big struggle and already reaching for the rubber mallet, but the plug comes off more easily than I expected. Dirty oil starts glugging out. Yoni lets out a little shriek as he fumbles for the bucket, and oil splashes on the front of his coveralls.

Something about that squeal is the funniest sound I've ever heard. I try not to laugh, but the more I try to press it inside, the more the laughter fights to bubble out. I fumble for the bottom of the bucket to keep it from tipping as it fills with oil.

"You jerk!" Yoni shouts. He's bright red. "You did that on purpose." He gives me a shove with the bucket between us. The oil sloshes, and some spills down the front of my coveralls.

"Are you nuts?" We're now both dirty and smudged with motor oil.

Mickey and Sara slide out from under the car to see what's going on. Sara's got a smear of dark grease on her upper lip that curls up on one side like a lopsided mustache.

"He opened the cap before I could get the bucket under." Yoni's face twists with anger. "He did it on purpose." If we weren't both holding the bucket with the dirty oil, I think he would have slugged me by now. But if either one of us lets go, we'll be drenched in sludge. Surprisingly, he's got enough brains to know that.

"It wasn't my fault," I say, through gritted teeth. "The cap was loose."

"All right now, settle down," Mickey says. "I'm sure it was all a mistake. We'll clean up at lunchtime."

Under Mickey's eye, we carefully set the bucket down together. Yoni opens and closes his fists, knuckles popping. I can feel the knots of tension tighten in my shoulders.

"Beni and I should work together," Sara quickly suggests. "Yoni can help you. That way there's an experienced person and a new one in each group."

Mickey, who's no fool, agrees, and we switch partners.

The knots in my shoulders remain.

At least Sara and I work well together. Sara has a great way of explaining things without sounding like she's lecturing or making me feel stupid. Yoni and Mickey don't have it quite as good, but other than a few whiny complaints, Yoni mostly shuts up and does what he's told.

When we break for lunch, Mickey points me to the small bathroom at the back of the shop. Once I'm there, I see my reflection in the mirror. My face is covered in long streaks of grease. I look like I've run into freshly painted prison bars. I snort at myself as I use a hand towel to scrub at my face and the black grease on my hands. Mickey has a special soap meant to clean off the dark grease. I get my face mostly clean, but dark stains stay under my fingernails and in the creases on the folds of my knuckles.

After telling Goliath to "watch the shop," Mickey takes us out for falafel nearby, at a one-room restaurant with three tables and mismatched vinyl-covered chairs. He treats us to orange soda as well. The restaurant might not be much to look at, but the falafel balls are hot and crispy, the tahini topping creamy and garlicky, and the pickled veggies tart. I wash it all down with a glug of soda.

We walk back to the shop on a lane so narrow and steep that it's just a flight of stairs. The old city was built long before cars and bicycles were forms of transportation.

By the afternoon, Mickey tells us to head home. There's a blackout in effect. No street lights will turn on once the sun sets. This is in case Syrian or Egyptian fighter planes are able to break through our air force's protection. Light is visible from far away at night. We don't want to give them an obvious target.

Sara heads to her uncle's house a few blocks away from the mechanic shop. She shoots me a sympathetic look on her way out. At least she'll get a break from Yoni.

Yoni and I walk back to the historic part of the city. We don't speak. I walk quickly, wanting to get home as soon as possible. The less time I spend with this creep, the better.

As we walk into my grandparents' house, I hear my mom on the phone.

"Poor little guy," she says in sympathy. "Subdermal hematoma is a big diagnosis for a little kid." She *hmmm*s in agreement at something. "Thanks for updating us. We'll keep Yoni as long as you need us to. He's no trouble at all."

Yoni and I both freeze in the entryway.

My mom hangs up. "Oh, hi, boys," she says brightly. "How was your day?" Her eyes widen as she takes in our greasy faces and dirty hands. "Straight to the bathroom," she says, pointing down the hall. "Don't touch the walls! Don't touch anything!"

"Ima," I say imploringly, "was that about Dor?"

"Yes," she says, but she's distracted. "We'll talk about it after you've washed up. Safta will lose her mind if she sees you. I'm serious—don't touch anything. What in God's name have you been doing?"

"Sara's uncle is a mechanic. His assistant is deployed. We helped him fix cars all day."

Her face softens for a moment as she realizes we weren't getting into trouble. I don't know what she was imagining. That we were vandalizing cars? Setting fires?

"That's great. I'm so glad you found a way to help. We had a couple of nice high schoolers stop by to deliver our mail."

"But what about Dor?" Yoni reminds her. "Is he okay?"

"He'll be fine!" she says in a cheerful tone.

"He'll *be* fine, or he *is* fine?" I ask.

"It'll work out," she says, evading my question.

"Are my parents coming to pick me up soon?" Yoni asks.

Her face clouds. "Well, that's a bit complicated. Dor needs to stay in the hospital for a few more days. They did a little procedure, and since he's so young, they're going to keep him under observation. You'll stay with us, of course."

"They had to operate on Dor?" I ask, the blood draining from my face. I feel hot and cold prickles all over me.

He's just a toddler. I picture his tiny body on a big hospital gurney. A surgeon with a scalpel. I feel sick.

"Oh, Beni, it's not your fault," my mom says, catching the look of horror on my face.

Yoni looks at me in surprise.

"Yes, it is," I say bitterly.

"No, it's not," Yoni says in the same bitter tone. "It's my fault."

Both my mom and I gape at him in shock.

"What?" I say, harshly. "You had nothing to do with it."

"Right, exactly," he says. His eyes narrow in loathing. But it's directed at himself. "If I hadn't taken so long to go back to the house to get the pacifier for Shoshi, I would've been there to help my mom."

"I'm the one who dropped him," I say angrily. "I'm the one who landed on him and hurt him!"

"At least you were with him!" Yoni yells at

me, his face turning red. His hands clench in fists at his side. He takes a step toward me.

"Stop! Listen to yourselves," my mother interrupts us. She steps between the two of us. "Neither one of you is to blame." She places a hand on each of our shoulders, as if to physically keep us apart. My mother is short and plump, but when she gets serious, it's as if she grows two feet taller. She is like a wall between us.

I glare at her in frustration, only to notice that Yoni is looking at her with a similar look of surly disbelief.

"I don't have the patience for this," she snaps. "Everyone had to run to the shelter. We were all in danger. Yoni, if you had tried to get back to your mother, you could have been killed. And Beni, if you hadn't helped Ronit, she wouldn't have been able to get to the shelter as fast as she did. Who knows what would have happened to her and Shoshi—and Dor." She gives us each a little shake, as if to knock some sense in. "So enough of this! We have enough real problems. We don't need to invent new ones."

She speaks with such forcefulness that I'm stunned into silence. I don't know what to think, what to believe. It suddenly strikes me how strange it is that Yoni and I are arguing over which of us is at fault, but we're not accusing each other—we're each trying to blame ourselves.

"You're not mad at me about Dor?" I ask Yoni.

"Are you a moron or something?" he asks. "You saved him. I'm the jerk who was inside the house, safe from the moment the shelling started."

"I tripped and fell on him. I hurt him." My voice cracks.

I feel my mom's hand on my hair. As quick as it rose, her temper has faded. She's back to being soft and kind. "Sweetheart, you did your best. Maybe your best wasn't perfect, but this is a war. We're only going to get through this if we help each other, and you did that. You risked your own life to help your neighbors. That's good enough."

It's typical of my mom to try to make me

feel better, whether I deserve it or not. Still, it confuses me that Yoni isn't mad at me.

I glance at him. Yoni's looking at the floor, shoulders slumped, his expression dull.

Maybe it shouldn't make a difference. I still have the bruises from where he and Ori beat me. He tormented Sara at school. He even kicked Goliath. But despite all that, the knots in my shoulders loosen a bit as I look at him. I know that look. Behind all the bragging and the big talk, Yoni is angry with himself.

"All right," my mom says. "Go to the shower and scrub down. If you stain Safta's wall, then we'll have an actual problem."

* * *

It's the end of the third day of the war. There's another movie on television.

After the movie, there's a short news update. The defense minister, David Elazar, comes on to brief the country. His deep, steady voice fills the living room. He has a very particular way of speaking, each word sharply pronounced and articulated. I can hear the determination and outrage in his voice. "We will break their bones," he says.

But there's no mention of any victories for us. No setbacks for the armies that crossed our borders.

The broadcast ends, and an episode of the American show *The Brady Bunch* comes on. It's hard to laugh along with the studio audience.

"Are we winning?" I ask out loud.

But no one in the room answers. My parents and grandparents sit facing the screen. The flickering light plays across their faces, their expressions wooden and worried.

The audience on TV laughs instead.

Chapter Nine

By the next day, Yoni and I are back in the auto shop, working together. We're not friends, but there's less tension between us. Yoni doesn't say one mean thing to Sara. Goliath steers clear of Yoni. We avoid spilling the oil on ourselves and the floor. We're getting better at this.

When the phone rings later that morning, Mickey answers. After a quick discussion, he tells the person on the phone, "I'm on my way."

We pause in our repairs.

"That was one of my favorite customers. She has a car that won't start. Want to come along and play auto detective?" he asks us.

Of course we do.

Goliath yips.

"No, buddy, not you," Mickey laughs. "You stay here. Guard the shop."

As if he understands, Goliath returns to his cushion, walks in a circle and settles down, chin on paws, watching the entrance of the shop.

We hop in Mickey's van, the back full of tools and spare parts, and drive across town.

There's a powder-blue sedan parked on the street in front of a three-story gray stucco apartment building. The car's hood is open, propped up by a metal stake. An older woman, her hair covered with a flowered silk kerchief tied under her chin, stands next to it.

"Mickey!" she says as soon as we pull up behind her car. "You're a dream. Thanks for coming so quickly."

She's wearing a polyester pantsuit in the same powder-blue shade as her car. A bright red scarf is jauntily tied around her neck.

"Of course, Penina," Mickey says, not batting an eye at her outfit. "I dropped everything and came over."

"Oh, Mickey!" She laughs, flirting.

Sara and I exchange looks. It's hard not to laugh.

"What happened this time?" Mickey asks and saunters over to the car.

"It wasn't me!" she insists. "I parked it last night. I didn't leave the lights on. I didn't leave the doors open. I don't know what's wrong with this car!"

"That's what I'm here for," he says soothingly. "Let's see what happens when I turn it on."

From the anxious look on her face, I don't know which worries Penina more, that the car will still be dead or that it will suddenly work for him when it didn't for her.

But when Mickey turns the key nothing happens. No coughing sound of the engine turning over, no muted roar as it comes to life.

Penina's face lights up with vindication. "You see!" she crows. "It's not me. It's the car's fault. It refuses to start." There's a tone of accusation in her voice, implying that the car is doing it on purpose, just to be difficult.

I can see Mickey trying to hide his grin.

Clearly, he wouldn't have been surprised if it had started when he tried.

"There are lots of reasons that a car won't start," he says, turning to us. "Our job is to go through them one by one."

We gather around the front of the car like medical students around a patient.

Mickey lists the possibilities: "Battery could be dead. Starter could be dead. Alternator could be dead. Bad ignition switch. Out of gas." He ticks each one on his fingers until he's got a hand full of reasons. "Let's see what we've got here."

"I filled the gas two days ago," Penina tells him. "After what happened last time, I don't let it go below half a tank."

Mickey nods approvingly. "Normally, with a dead car, it's the battery," he says. "The engine was silent when I turned the key, which means it's probably not the starter. When there's a problem with the starter, there's usually a clicking noise or a faint starting sound. But you never know."

He tilts his head and leans farther down into the hood of the car.

"Hmmm," he says. "This is interesting."

"What?" Penina asks fearfully. "Was it something I did?"

"Not at all," he says. Under his breath, he mutters, "Not this time." He straightens and waves us closer. "Come here, kids, I want you to see this."

One by one, the three of us duck under the overhanging hood and look where he's pointing.

Instead of the normal tangle of smooth wires, there are shredded bits of wire coating, and several of the wires have been severed.

"Who would do this?" I ask. Visions of assassins tampering with Penina's car dance through my head. I look at her again, reassessing. Could she be some kind of spy or government agent?

"Not who," Mickey says mysteriously. He reaches in again and pulls something out, holding it between his fingers. "What."

Between his blackened, grease-stained fingers are several gray fluffy strands.

"Fur?" Yoni asks.

"Fur?" Penina echoes weakly.

"You've got mice," Mickey says cheerfully. "It was cold last night. You pulled in here and parked your nice warm car. They decided to hop in and make themselves comfortable. It could be worse—I've seen an engine intake filled with acorns. Once I even had a client with a whole nest in his air intake duct. You can't imagine the smell. They pee and poop in their nests like you wouldn't believe."

"That's disgusting!" Sara cries.

"I hate mice," Penina says. "But at least it wasn't my fault." She looks at him hopefully. "It wasn't . . . right?"

"Not your fault at all," he reassures her. "It happens from time to time. Not much you can do to stop it. Some people sprinkle cayenne pepper, but you better be careful where you do that, or you'll get a face full of it when you turn on your heat."

"Oy vey!" she exclaims. "Can you fix it?"

"Are you kidding me?" Mickey says, clutching his chest, his honor as a mechanic insulted. "Of course I can fix it. For now, I'll splice the wires and wrap them together in electrical tape. But after the holiday, swing by the shop, and I'll replace the wires."

"You're a dream, Mickey," she says, her face brightening.

Mickey disconnects the battery. He shows us how to pull back the plastic coating on the chewed wires, exposing the copper wires underneath. Once there's enough to handle on both ends, he twists them tightly together and wraps the exposed metal with black electrical tape. Finally he reconnects the battery.

"There," he says. "Let's see if it starts now. Sara, you want to try?" He holds out the key to Sara.

She scampers into the front seat, her head barely clearing the dashboard. She inserts the key, and with a twist of her wrist, the engine roars to life.

We all clap and cheer.

Mickey smiles and shrugs. "It's only a temporary fix," he warns Penina. "Be sure to come back after Sukkot."

"I will," she says. "But can I drive it now?"

"Should be fine," Mickey says. "Where are you off to?"

"I'm driving down to Haifa to see my daughter for the holiday."

"There's no hurry. You have plenty of time," Mickey says. With the evening curfew still in effect, she'll need to be off the road by dark.

"But I knitted a hat," Penina says, holding up a cozy-looking brown lump. "They're saying the boys up at the Golan didn't bring enough warm gear. It's freezing there at night. I stayed up half the night finishing this one. I want to drop it off before they send the box out."

Even though the days are warm, at night the temperatures fall sharply. And it isn't just Yuval's unit that rushed to the front. Most of the fighting troops didn't pack extra food, and they didn't pack extra gear either.

"We're making a care package too," Sara mentions. "We're sending socks and underwear, and we bought a lot of candy."

"That's great," Penina says warmly. "We all need to help! Do you know, I always make a point to give rides to hitchhiking soldiers. It's the least I can do."

"Is that to help them or to keep you company?" Mickey teases.

"Both!" she chuckles. "I call that a win-win!"

She hops in the car. With a toot of her horn, she pulls away, scraping her bumper on the curb on her way out. She veers around another parked car, barely missing clipping the side mirror, and disappears around the bend.

We pass a small grocery store on our way back to the shop. Through the glass windows at the front of the store, I can see a thick crowd of women jostling for groceries. The stores can't resupply their goods. Some of the shelves are bare, and Sukkot is coming.

Back at the shop, we're all quiet. Even though Penina was so cheerful, her knitted hat reminded us of the war. There are moments when I forget that I'm not here on a vacation. Our soldiers are out there fighting, day and night, and maybe getting hurt to protect us. I can tell Sara is thinking about her brother. I'm worried about Motti. The Egyptians, the Syrians, and the troops from other Arab nations who've arrived to help them outnumber us two to one. A woolen hat isn't going to protect us from that.

* * *

The next afternoon I find Safta in the kitchen, flipping through a stained cookbook, frustrated. I've left Yoni in the living room, reading an old comic book.

"Can't make apple cake," she says, ticking off her usual repertoire of holiday baking. "That needs three eggs. Can't make cheesecake. It will use up all the butter I have left, and who knows when more will come in. Can't make chocolate cake; we're running low on flour." She closes the book and replaces it on the shelf.

"Well, Beni," she says with a sigh, "we'll have to adjust this year. I still have a loaf of honey cake in the freezer. I can make a syrup from our fig jam. You like fig syrup, right?" She waits for my nod. "And if you and your friend go pick some pomegranates from Miriam's yard, then we'll have a fine dessert."

She smiles at me, but her heart's not in it. She and my mom keep picking fights with each other, arguing over every little thing. The breakfast dishes. The right way to fold the laundry. My dad's smoking.

"That sounds great, Safta," I say.

She ruffles my hair. "You're a good boy, Beni," she says.

But I'm not being nice about dessert because I'm "good." All I can think about is Motti. Sukkot starts tonight, and he said he'd be home by now. But he's not.

Who cares about cake, anyway?

Chapter Ten

Sukkot, a harvest festival since biblical times, lasts for a week. We celebrate by building small huts with thatched roofs called sukkahs where we eat our meals. People decorate their sukkahs with paper chains, bundles of wheat, and other homemade decorations.

Small sukkahs have popped up on balconies and in courtyards, little testaments to the fact that life goes on. There's a war and people are dying, but the holidays still come and people still observe them.

The news has started getting more specific about what's going on. No victories for us, other than the fact that the entire country hasn't been invaded. There's setback after setback. Rumors swirl about heavy casualties. No one thinks the war will be over soon. Officials have stopped saying, "We'll break their bones." It's our bones that are breaking.

The mood in the city drops. Before, people were tense but eager for the whole thing to be over already. Now there's a sinking realization that this won't be fast. It won't be easy. There will be many casualties on both sides. Deaths.

On the fourth day of Sukkot, my mom gets off the phone with Yoni's mother with good news. The procedure to relieve the swelling in Dor's brain was successful. He's been released from the hospital. They're on their way to get Yoni.

"Dor's good as new," my mom says brightly. Is there something in her tone that says she thinks otherwise? It's hard for me to tell.

Yoni doesn't have much to pack. Just a pair of pants and a shirt borrowed from the kids at Kibbutz Lavi. He's been sleeping in an old shirt of my grandfather's, which he leaves folded on the bed in the loft. My parents bought him a toothbrush, and he carefully wraps it in a napkin to take with him.

I get to sleep in the loft now. But I'm surprised to feel a little sad that Yoni's leaving. We're not enemies anymore, although we're not quite friends either. I'm also nervous about seeing Dor again. I want to see with my own eyes that he's okay. But will he burst into tears when he sees me? Scream in terror? Do his parents hate me?

Yoni and I sit on the front steps outside my grandparents' front door, waiting for his family to arrive. It's another beautiful day, the sky sharp and blue with fat, happy clouds. I steal a sideways glance at him. He seems tense, picking at a small hangnail on his thumb. He's been fiddling with it so much that it's all pink with a small dot of red blood, but he doesn't stop.

Even though he's been staying with us for days, we've steered clear of any difficult topics. I haven't asked about his dad. He doesn't mention the constant sniping between my mom and my grandmother. And neither one of us talks about Dor. Just cars, food, helping Mickey at the shop, and whatever show's on television. I suddenly want to ask him so many questions, but before I can start, a car pulls into the narrow lane in front of the house.

Out spill Yoni's parents.

"They're here!" I shout through the open front door of my grandparents' house, rising to my feet.

My parents and grandparents leave their perch by the television, where they've been waiting for a news update.

My dad and Baruch, Yoni's dad, embrace, clapping each other on the back.

My mom and Ronit hug as well. Everyone exclaims their greetings, their thanks, their updates on the latest rumors and the state of our moshav.

"The Syrians have been pushed back," Baruch tells my dad. "A few of the guys and I are going there in a few days to check it out. You should come."

My dad agrees, though I catch the worried look on my mom's face.

"Let's see Dor," my mom says, changing the subject. "We've been worried about him."

"He fell asleep on the ride," Ronit says. "He and the baby."

My mom peers in the back seat and smiles.

"Sleep is the best medicine," she says. I've heard her say that before. Usually when she wants me to go to bed.

"I missed you so much, sweetie," Yoni's mom says to him. She gives Yoni a big hug, rocking him from side to side in her arms. He's a head taller than her, but she's treating him like a baby. I can see Yoni's cheeks stained with color.

I edge toward the car. The windows are rolled up and at first all I can see is my reflection looking back at me.

"I hope Yoni's been behaving," his dad says darkly.

"Of course," my mom hurries to say. "He's a great kid. Very polite."

I peer through the window, cupping my hands around my face to block the light. I can just make out Dor, slumped to one side against the window, fast asleep. He looks normal, maybe a little pale, a little thin. It's hard to tell.

"I'm glad to hear it." Baruch hitches up his pants. "Beni," he says, his voice low and rough. I guiltily jump away from the car, as if I've done something wrong. My heart knocks in my chest. There's something so cruel in his face. "My family and I owe you a huge debt. You saved Dor. We will never forget it."

I swallow and blink in surprise. My parents and grandparents beam at me.

"I, ah, I'm glad he's okay."

"Beni's been so worried about Dor," my mom says.

There's a soft, kind look on Ronit's face. "He'll be fine, Beni," she says. "Kids are resilient, they bounce back and—"

"We've imposed long enough," Yoni's dad says sharply, interrupting his wife. "Grab your things, Yoni." He turns back to my dad and tells him, "I'm dropping the family in Haifa. Then I'm going to Nafah. As soon as they give the green light, I'm going to the moshav. I'll call you as soon as I hear anything."

My dad nods his thanks.

Yoni climbs into the back of the car and they leave.

"Strange family," my mom says as their car disappears around the bend. She puts her arm around my shoulder and gives me a squeeze. "I'm glad Yoni could stay with us. I think he could really use a friend."

It occurs to me that she's probably right. Having Baruch as a dad can't be easy. Somehow, I bet that Baruch's definition of being a man is different from Motti's or Mickey's. To him, it isn't about taking care of other people, and it isn't about being good at a job. To Baruch, and to a lot of other people, being a man means one thing: If someone punches you, you punch back harder.

* * *

The war drags on.

Sukkot's over, and there's still no end in sight.

Every day, my parents' mood sinks lower. While the fighting seems to have turned in our favor, casualties keep mounting. My mom and grandmother knit hats. They avoid each other by alternating sitting by the radio in the kitchen and in front of the television in the living room, wherever the other one isn't sitting. As they wait for the hourly updates, they stitch row after row of brown wool. In between songs, the radio announcer often reads short messages from families to their soldiers—words of love and encouragement to lift their morale.

Whenever they have to cross paths, my mom and grandmother bicker. I hadn't realized how much Yoni's presence kept them on good behavior. Soon, my dad is drawn into the fights.

Behind the closed door of my dad's child-hood bedroom, I hear my mom accusing my dad of always taking his mother's side. I overhear my dad hiss that he wouldn't need to if she'd only try to get along.

"I can't take it anymore!" my mom shouts at my dad.

"Sweetheart . . ." He draws out the syllables. He's trying to sound calm, but it comes out patronizing.

"No!" she cuts him off, out of patience. "I have nothing left to give. It's too much." Her voice drops, and I can't hear what she says next. I hear my dad's low murmur, soothing her.

"I can't stop thinking about Giddi," she says brokenly. I haven't heard her call Gideon by his childhood nickname in years. "What if Motti—"

"It won't be like that," my dad says forcefully, not letting her finish. "You can't even think it. He'll be fine."

I jump back from their door at the sound of footsteps. My grandmother stands in the hallway. Our eyes meet. She's clearly heard my parents. She looks stricken, as if overhearing my mom's fear—all of our fear—spoken out loud makes it scarier for all of us. Like if one of us stops pretending that everything is fine, the whole charade will crumble. Has she been picking fights with my mom to distract herself from that bigger worry?

"Come with me, Beni," she says quietly. "Saba wants someone to play chess with. You need to trounce him; he's getting much too big for his britches."

My parents' voices drop again, their words lost in whispers and long silences.

"Sure," I tell my grandmother, trying for a smile.

I walk away from my perch by their door, my heart heavy and sad. I wish so badly that Motti were here. What if my parents fight so much they end up getting a divorce? But other than magically bringing Motti home safely, I don't know what I could possibly do to ease the strain.

My grandfather and I play chess. The radio drones on in the background. *Hello Gaby, from your wife, Liora, who loves you.*

As I ponder my next move, I suddenly get an idea.

"What are you smiling at?" my grandfather asks. "Your queen's in danger. That's nothing to smile about."

"You'll see," I say mysteriously.

I'm able to sacrifice a knight and save my queen. Saba grunts and rubs his upper lip as he studies the board.

At dinner that night, I share my idea. "We should send Motti a message on the radio," I say.

My parents sit up straighter, with looks of happy surprise.

"That's a great idea!" my mom says. "Why didn't we think of that sooner?"

"What should we say?" my dad wonders.

"Ummm, should we tell him we're with Saba and Safta in Safed?" I suggest. "He might think we're back at the moshav by now."

"No," my dad says, shaking his head. "We don't know when they'll read the message on the radio—it could take days, and I don't want to confuse him. We could say *Hello from your parents and brother.*"

My mom and I make a face.

"That's pretty boring," I say.

We toss around some different ideas, but nothing seems quite right. It has to be short, or the announcer won't read it. He must get hundreds of requests every day.

My grandmother has been sitting on the couch, knitting silently all this time. Out of the blue, she speaks. "*Motti, everything is fine with us. Be strong. We'll see you soon.*"

We fall silent and look at her in surprise.

"It's perfect," my mom says after a moment. "That's what we'll say."

A look passes between them. While my grandmother never lost a son to war, she lost her oldest grandson, and she sent her own boys into danger more than once. Like my mom, she knows what it's like to worry. For a moment, the tension between them vanishes. It's like they've suddenly remembered that they're on the same side. My grandmother nods and rises from the couch. As she passes my mom, she places a hand on her shoulder. My mom covers my grandmother's hand with hers.

My dad and I share a smile. A truce has been declared.

* * *

The first death notices appear in the town square. In the past, the military always waited until the end of the war to announce deaths. But since so many soldiers have died, and the war is still going with no end in sight, they've broken tradition and started telling families. Like mushrooms after a rain, soon after the first appears, there's another and another. My mother averts her eyes when she walks by. She stays in her room more and more. Sometimes I can hear her crying.

With the garbage collectors gone, trash overflows in the streets. Local high school students organize and do what they can to move the trash to the local dump. Our mail is delivered by a series of sixteen- and seventeen-year-olds.

I'm walking back from Mickey's shop when a high schooler pulling a handcart stuffed with mail passes by my grandparents' house and hands me a stack of envelopes. I shuffle through the bills and letters from my grandparents' friends, my black-rimmed nails leaving small smears of grease on the envelopes, until I catch sight of a pale green, military-issued postcard on top. My heart leaps for joy at the sight of Motti's familiar scrawl.

"We got a letter from Motti!" I shout, running into the house.

"What?" my mom says, leaping off the couch. My grandparents are half a step behind her.

"Here!" I wave the postcard.

They all rush over, and we huddle around the small rectangle.

Stuck in traffic, Motti writes. *All is well. Not much to write, so here's a doodle instead. Love you all—Motti.*

It's dated Sunday, the day after Yom Kippur. He's sketched a turtle and a snail in a race. There's sweat flying off them, and they're eyeing each other with menace. The turtle has one leg in the air, about to take a step, and the snail's antennae are straining forward. But it's obvious that neither one is moving anywhere fast. The finish line is off in the distance.

My mom and I share a smile at the silly drawing.

We've heard reports that in the first few days of the war, there were epic traffic jams of military vehicles heading to the front. Trips that should have taken six or seven hours took twenty-four hours or longer.

"When does Abba get back?" I ask. He left for the day to check in at Nafah and see what he can do to help.

"Soon," she says. "What a great surprise for him when he gets home."

I'm happy for the rest of the day, glancing at the postcard every once in a while. I hope Sara gets one from Yuval soon. There's nothing like hearing from your family, even if the message was written days ago, to make you feel like everything will be okay. It feels like winning the lottery.

My parents don't fight that night. The truce between my mom and my grandmother holds. My mom compliments Safta on the soup, and my grandmother quickly explains the recipe— their version of a peace offered and accepted.

But strangely, that night, as I lie in my loft, I'm struck by a feeling of sadness.

I miss Motti so much. I wish he were lying next to me in the loft. If he were here, he'd make sure that our parents stop fighting for good. If he were here, he could make my grandmother laugh and distract her from all the things my mom has been doing to annoy her. He can fix everything. But I can't.

For the first time in a long time, I really think about my brother Gideon. I was six when he died. He would have been twenty-four years old now. An adult. I picture him looking like Motti, but taller and with darker hair. Long out of the military, maybe married. Maybe I would have been an uncle.

It seems unbearably sad. Gideon never got to have that. No university. No wedding. Just a white tombstone and visits on his birthday and Memorial Day. He was robbed of so much.

But here's the thing—we were robbed too.

I'm rocked by a wave of grief. He's been gone for six years, but I still miss him.

Chapter Eleven

After Simchat Torah, the holiday that comes at the end of Sukkot, school starts again at Kibbutz Lavi. My parents and Sara's parents decide we can't neglect our studies any longer. When I try to protest, my dad cuts me off.

"Nothing is more important than education," my dad says. "When the Nazis rounded Jews up into concentration camps, the first thing they did was outlaw reading and writing. Why?" he asks rhetorically. I know better than to answer. "Because they knew that knowledge is powerful. Never allow anyone to take that away from you." This is one of his most common lectures. "Knowledge is power. And studying is where knowledge comes from. Are we clear?"

We're clear.

From Safed, the distance to Kibbutz Lavi is actually shorter than it is from our moshav. The problem is the buses. The morning bus that normally runs from Safed to Kibbutz Lavi is thirty minutes late. Most of the bus drivers have deployed to fight in the war. The older drivers are doing their best but failing to manage the workload.

When Sara and I finally make it to school, we find the classroom has been transformed. Instead of the normal neat rows of desks, everything has been pushed aside to make room on the floor. Small groups of students sit cross-legged with mounds of papers in front of them. Everyone pauses in their work as we walk in.

Sara blushes, her shoulders hunched up around her ears. I almost forgot how much Sara hates to be the center of attention.

"*Mes enfants!*" Morah Yvette exclaims as soon as she sees us, lapsing into French in her excitement. "Welcome back!"

Students return to their work, and the crinkling from so many pages being turned and shuffled at the same time fills the room.

Yvette rushes over to hug us. She presses a kiss to one cheek and then the other in her French way, and now I'm the one blushing, with my shoulders up around my ears.

"I'm so glad you came to school!" she continues. She holds me by the shoulders, pressing with her hands as if to push her happiness into me. After I nod, she does the same to Sara.

"What's going on?" I ask, gesturing to the students on the floor. "What's the assignment?"

"Ah, yes," she says with a pleased expression. "A new project. Since we were all caught by surprise by this situation, finding ourselves in the middle of a war, I decided that your task today is to sort through the news and create an outline for what has happened so far. I expect a map with diagrams of Egyptian, Syrian, and Israeli military movements."

I can barely hide my surprise. I thought she'd be drilling us on the ancient Punic Wars or the parts of a cell. But this is actually interesting. I've been following the news, of course, but not closely enough to know many details. Mostly

I've tried to stay out of the house and out of my parents' way.

"I've collected multiple editions every day since Yom Kippur." She gestures proudly to the stacks of newspapers that the other students are reading. "After you establish the chronological events, I want an analysis from you of how the war is going. Join one of the groups and start reading."

I scan the room, looking for a group to join. Yoni and Ori are working together in the back corner. Everyone seems to be in groups of three to four, other than the two of them. I'm not sure if Yoni wants to be my friend now that we're back in school, but I'm not scared of him. Besides, there's no other group to join. Sara and I head to the back of the room.

Ori rolls his eyes when he sees us and turns to Yoni, ready to say something mean. But Yoni nods at us in a friendly way. Ori suddenly looks uncertain.

"Start here," Yoni says, pointing to a stack on his right. "We've put the issues in chrono-logical order. There was no newspaper on Yom

Kippur, of course, so the first news about the war got printed on October 7."

I scan the first headline: ISRAEL PREPARES FOR YOM KIPPUR, BUT EGYPT AND SYRIA PREPARE FOR WAR.

RESERVE SOLDIERS MOBILIZED, reads another headline.

I knew we had a lot of reservists who activated, but I didn't realize that overnight, 200,000 Israeli civilians had rushed to join their old military units. No wonder it's felt like the country is falling apart. One-sixteenth of the population has been away fighting.

I read several articles about tank battles that raged in the central region of the Golan. My moshav is just south of that. There is almost no doubt that Syrians reached my neighborhood. I shiver to think of it, remembering the endless shelling on Yom Kippur.

Quickly, the news reports turn even darker.

By October 9, a retired general is quoted saying, "This is not going to be a short war." The headline reads, A COUNTER OFFENSE IN THE SINAI FAILS.

I try not to think of Motti, who is likely stationed in the Sinai. He's in a tank, I tell myself. He's bulletproof.

There're reports of the Israeli forts along the Suez Canal being completely overrun. In the first minute of the war, 10,000 shells fell on the Israeli lines in the Sinai. With fewer than 500 Israeli men stationed in forts along the Suez Canal, the Egyptians sent over 23,000 soldiers in two hours. Our soldiers didn't stand a chance. The vast majority of the men stationed in the forts are dead, captured, or missing.

Up north, the situation isn't much better. At the start of the war, there were 177 Israeli tanks in the Golan. The Syrians attacked with 1,400 tanks. Two hundred Israeli soldiers faced some 40,000 Syrian troops.

There are several articles about a young lieutenant named Zvika Greengold who single-handedly defended Nafah against Syrian tanks. I pause for a moment, blinking in shock. The military headquarters for the Golan Heights, the one we're in contact with all the time, was nearly overrun. The only thing that saved it was one lieutenant in a tank. Because Zvika knew the Syrians could overhear him on the radio, when the headquarters asked which unit he belonged to and how many tanks he had with him, he said he was part of Force Zvika and that he couldn't say how many tanks he had. In the chaos and confusion of the early part of the war, the Israeli commanders assumed he must be part of a large force they somehow missed in their calculations. The Syrians, overhearing them, thought the same thing. Zvika Greengold fought for thirty hours straight, holding back hundreds of Syrian tanks.

It isn't until the fifth day of the war that the headlines read, SYRIANS PUSHED BACK TO BORDER.

Yoni and Ori have the newspapers from the next two days. Rather than wait for them to finish, I dig through the mess of papers at our feet and jump to the days ahead.

More bad news. On October 14, two days ago, Egyptian forces broke through Israel's second line of defense to reach the Mitla Pass, one of the few roads that run through the huge desert, a critical military location. Hundreds of tanks took part in the largest tank battle since World War II. In the end, the Egyptians were pushed back. Some 250 Egyptian tanks were destroyed. Israel lost twenty tanks.

I set down the paper, my face prickling with heat, my stomach churning. The math assaults me. Two hundred and fifty Egyptian tanks. Four crew members per tank. One thousand men. On the Israeli side: Twenty tanks. Four crew members per tank. Eighty men. Men someone loved, men someone worried about, men who are not coming home.

Today, October 16, ten days after the war started, the morning edition of the paper reported that Israeli paratroopers are crossing the Suez Canal into Egypt. Though the fighting is still raging, it seems the momentum of the war has turned in our favor.

But that doesn't mean we're in good shape. The IDF has already announced the names of 656 soldiers killed. Hundreds more have been captured as war prisoners. And we aren't done yet. More will be killed. More will be captured.

I picture Motti, with his curly hair and pale eyes, tired, grimy, fighting for his life. I feel sick with worry.

"So where did you stay last week?" I ask Ori, desperate for a distraction from my thoughts. "Sara and Yoni and I were in Safed."

"Why do I care where you were?" Ori says, rolling his eyes. He looks over at Yoni with a snort as if to say, *Can you believe this guy?*

I brace myself, expecting Yoni to grunt and say something rude.

But Yoni doesn't. Ori blinks in confusion.

Sara sits very still. We're all waiting to see what Yoni will do.

But Yoni doesn't seem to want to do anything. He keeps looking at the paper in his hands, flipping through the pages. There's a cartoon of a man listening to the radio, dreaming about a secret weapon.

"Ori stayed here at the kibbutz. His mom had to be at the hospital," Yoni says without looking up.

There's a moment of silence as Ori digests this new reality in which I'm not an outcast.

"What's wrong with your mom?" Sara asks.

"Nothing. She's a nurse," Ori says. He's holding a paper from a few days ago with the headline: UNITED JEWISH APPEAL IN NEW YORK RAISES $30 MILLION IN ONE DAY TO HELP ISRAEL.

"What is she saying about the hospital?" Sara asks. She pretends like it's a casual question, but her hands grip the newspaper so strongly that the paper crinkles. "Are there a lot of soldiers? Has she seen any tankers?"

Sara's family has yet to receive a single postcard from Yuval. They've left radio messages and reached out to other families from his brigade, but no one has any information. It's as if the Golan has swallowed the entire brigade whole.

"Sure," Ori says. "The tankers mostly come in with burns. There's not much you can do for that."

The thin newspaper rips in Sara's hands.

Ori doesn't look up from his lap. He's lost in his own thoughts. He opens his mouth, then closes it. Takes a breath, then lets it out. His eyes shift to the side.

"Just say it," I say, exasperated.

"She's treating Syrian prisoners," he blurts out.

The color drains from Sara's face, except for her dark eyes, magnified behind her glasses.

"What?" Yoni says. He has that tight look on his face, the one that shows up right before he loses his temper. "After what they did to us?"

Ori flushes. With his long neck and his long eyelashes, his face blotchy with red and white spots, he is one frustrated giraffe. "It's her job."

"My brother is out there," Sara says, her voice choked and strained. "Risking his life to protect us from them. You know what the Syrians do to our pilots? They torture them. And your mom is *helping* them?"

"She says . . ." Ori looks down at his hands. His fingernails have been bitten to the quick, the skin around them red and raw. "She says that she hopes there's a Syrian nurse out there taking care of our soldiers." He looks at me, misery and guilt on his face. He thinks that I hate his mom for helping the people trying to kill us. He knows about what happened to Gideon. They all do.

My first thought is how unfair it all is. Gideon wasn't killed by the Syrians, but he was killed by someone who didn't want Israel to exist, just like the Syrians. And we keep fighting and killing and getting killed, just to prove again and again that we do exist—that we will continue to exist.

It's hard. It's hard not to hate someone who hates you. It's hard not to hurt someone who's hurt you.

"Your mom sounds like a nice person," I finally say.

"She is. My mom is the best mom in the whole world." He says it defiantly, like we're going to disagree.

Sara, Yoni, and I exchange looks. *My* mom is the best mom in the whole world, but I decide not to argue with Ori. I guess Sara and Yoni are on the same page, because we all fall silent.

What are they like, these people who hate us so much that they're willing to die to make us vanish? I'm used to thinking of them as "the enemy"—as something different from us. It's strange to think of them wounded, hurting, and scared.

"Everyone, please collect your newspapers and bring them to the front of the room," Morah Yvette announces, interrupting our thoughts. "We will continue to work on our current events project. But for now, take out your history books. It's time to review the Punic Wars before your test on Wednesday."

Chapter Twelve

On October 26, twenty-one days after the war started, a ceasefire is declared. The fighting has stopped.

To the north, the Syrians have been pushed out of the Golan. Our tanks came within forty kilometers of Damascus, their capital. To the south, it's more complicated. The ceasefire left Israeli forces in Egypt and Egyptian forces in Israel, like that black and white yin-yang symbol I've seen in a book.

You could call it a win, since we still have a country. But even if we technically won, it doesn't feel like it.

A total of 2,600 Israelis killed. Seven thousand wounded. Hundreds captured as prisoners.

Every town center in Israel has a wall papered with black-bordered death notices. The newspapers are full of more black-bordered announcements for fallen soldiers. My dad's cousin has lost her son. My grandmother's hairdresser has lost her husband. A different cousin's boyfriend was killed. It feels like every day, the phone rings with someone telling my parents about another funeral, another shiva.

We move out of my grandparents' house and return to the moshav.

Our moshav is a mess: the fields scorched, cars burned. The shelling damaged a lot of the houses, including ours. The impact of a nearby mortar hit shattered all our windows. There's been some looting and graffiti on our street, but our home was left alone, probably because the blown-out windows made it look structurally unsafe.

The structure of the house is actually okay, but inside there's broken glass on everything. When I enter my room, my bed looks like it's covered in glittering frost, but it's all glass. We spend days sweeping, mopping, wiping down, and shaking out every centimeter inside. We throw away the food that rotted while we were gone. My mom finds a twisted piece of shrapnel embedded in the kitchen cabinet like an arrow. She digs it out, and it leaves a gouge in the thin wood.

I'm outside watering the new flowers in our front garden while my mom is chatting with our next-door neighbor, Miriam, and admiring Miriam's six-month-old baby. We all freeze as a military jeep pulls up.

Two carefully dressed soldiers step out. They walk with purpose up the narrow path that leads to our neighbor's house, toward my mom.

I was six years old when soldiers came to tell us that Gideon had fallen. Until this moment, if anyone had asked me, I would have said that I didn't remember anything about that day. I was only a little kid. But as soon as I see the jeep, I start to remember. As if the past and the present are merging in some awful loop, sudden memories flood me. A knock on the door that woke me from a nap. Stumbling into our living room to find my mother screaming at two soldiers to go away, to leave and take their horrible news with them. I remember terror and fury. I remember running to my mom, hugging her legs, yelling at the soldiers to leave her alone. I didn't understand that they hadn't hurt her on purpose. They had done nothing wrong. Nothing except tell my mom that her son was dead.

My heart is racing as memories and current events crash into each other. For a moment, I don't know where I am, whose news this is. I feel dizzy and sick.

"Miriam Bourski?" one of them asks. Our neighbor cries out, her hand flying to her mouth.

"I'm sorry to tell you that your husband, Nadav, has fallen."

My mother has an arm around Miriam, holding her up. Miriam clutches her baby, as if to protect him from the news. I drop the watering can, the water sloshing over the side, and hurry away, like their tragedy might be contagious.

My mother stays with Miriam for hours, taking care of her and the baby until Miriam's parents arrive from Naharia. When my mom finally comes home that night, she is pale and drained. She doesn't even make dinner.

"I have a terrible headache," she says, barely walking in a straight line as she heads directly to the bedroom. "I need to lie down."

My dad and I eat hardboiled eggs and tinned sardines on crackers. The empty chairs at our kitchen table seem to suck the words out of both of us.

* * *

Because it's only a ceasefire, fighting could restart at any time. Our troops are still in Egypt, camped out 101 kilometers outside of Cairo. The Egyptian Third Army is on our side of the canal, surrounded but still needing new shipments of food, water, and basic supplies. This means that none of our soldiers will be coming home. They stay activated and deployed. The shortages at the stores continue.

Some families we know have heard from their soldiers, but not us. I run to the post office every day to check our box, but there's nothing from Motti. On the other hand, we haven't been told he's been killed either. No black-bordered announcements bear his name. No other military jeeps drive to our moshav.

"He's okay," my dad reassures us. He says it forcefully. He says it with conviction. He says it as if he can make it so.

I'm scared for Motti. I'm scared soldiers will come to our door and tell us he's died. I'm scared of the math that tells me thousands of families are getting knocks on their doors. I'm scared that army personnel are slowly making their way down the list and they just haven't gotten to us yet.

At night, my stomach cramps so badly that I can't sleep. I lie in my bed, curled on my side, my pillow pressed against my belly. My thoughts race back and forth on the same track. Is he okay? Where is he? Why hasn't he written? Is he okay? Where is he? Why hasn't he written? Is he okay?

In the meantime, there's a lot to do.

A week after we move back home, my dad and I are still busy helping rebuild the irrigation systems that have been broken, the long pipes snapped in multiple places from the shelling. The weather's turned cool, but I'm sweaty and covered in smears of dirt. With most of the able-bodied men still deployed, the repairs fall to Yoni, Ori, me, and our fathers—though Baruch isn't here most of the time. He's serving as the local messenger, connecting the various spread-out Golan communities with the military base. We need all the help we can get, but I'm not exactly sorry he isn't around.

At one point, Baruch does swing by, kicking up dust behind his small truck. My dad and Ori's dad use his visit as a reason to take a break from the labor, pressing their hands to their lower backs and stretching with groans.

Ori, Yoni, and I take a break too, sprawling on the dirt while our dads talk in low voices.

Later, over dinner, my dad fills us in on the latest gossip. "They're saying at Nafah that the south didn't have any mail service for the first two weeks. It was a miracle Motti was able to mail that first postcard. He must have left it at the forward operating base. After that, he wouldn't have had a chance to send us anything."

"Did you ask him about Motti's unit?" my mom asks. "Where are they now?"

My parents have speculated that Motti might be across the Suez Canal, in Egypt. There's a fair-sized force there, our yin in their yang, and that would explain the long silence.

My dad makes a face. "Nafah is the northern command, and Motti's under the southern command. They don't know the specifics here in the north."

My mom gives him a look.

"I know, sweetheart," he says. "I'll keep asking."

"Sara's family hasn't gotten anything from her brother either," I mention. "And he's stationed in the Golan."

They nod, silently acknowledging that it's a mess, that there's reason to be hopeful. But the worry stays, hanging like wisps of smoke in the room.

"Some of the women I know are going to Haifa tomorrow," my mom says. "I think I'll go too."

Silence. My dad and I stare at her.

She taps her nail against the kitchen table in a quick, agitated rhythm.

"They've set up huge rooms with photos from Arab newspapers." Neither Egypt nor Syria has released any names or said how many Israeli soldiers they have. But the Arab-language papers have published photos of captured Israelis. Foreign journalists were allowed a few visits as well. "The military is encouraging people to come look through the photos to see if they can recognize the captured soldiers. They're trying to make prisoner lists."

I've known all along that some of our soldiers have been taken as prisoners, just like I know we've been holding some Egyptian and Syrian prisoners. But I've never stopped to think about who those prisoners are. Someone's husband, someone's son, someone's brother.

I feel my face prickle with heat. She hasn't come out and said it. So I do.

"You think Motti was captured?" I ask. "You think he's a prisoner?"

"Beni, we don't know," my dad says.

"It doesn't hurt to look," my mom says at the same time. "Maybe I can help identify someone, even if it isn't Motti."

A thick silence falls. It's just the three of us sitting around the table, a lopsided number. The chair across from me where Motti usually sits is empty. We used to be five people around the table. Then four. Now only three.

There's a photo in our living room of Gideon, Motti, and me, taken a few months before Gideon died. Gideon's in the middle with Motti on one side and me on the other. His arms are around both of us, sort of tucking us under his wings. There's a gap in my smile where my two front teeth are missing.

People have told me that I resemble Gideon. As I grow older without him, I can see how my face is changing to look more like the face of the young man he was.

There's a more recent photo too. It's the last one taken in Jerusalem before we moved here. Motti and I are standing by the tree in the courtyard of our old building in Jerusalem. Motti's arm is slung around my neck. He must have said something right before my dad snapped the photo, because I've turned my head to look at him, both of us grinning at his joke.

Gideon was eighteen when he died, the same age as Motti now.

Will there soon be a photo of only me? I can't bear the thought.

Be safe, Motti, I pray. *Be safe.*

"I'm coming with you," I tell my mom.

My parents exchange glances.

"Are you sure, sweetie?" my mom asks. "It's going to be a long, hard day."

"Two pairs of eyes are better than one," I argue, trying to sound tough and worldly. I can sense their unvoiced worry. They know about my stomachaches. They know about my sleepless nights. "Besides, it'll get me out of field duty," I say. "Anything's better than digging ditches."

* * *

The next day, my mom and I and several other women from the Golan catch a bus to Haifa.

We disembark at Masaryk Square. The road is full of cars, the sidewalks packed with pedestrians. Haifa is Israel's third-largest city, after

Tel Aviv and Jerusalem. It's been a while since I've been around so much traffic. There's a large movie theater at one corner of the busy intersection. It's showing a James Bond movie starring the British movie star Roger Moore. I wish we could stay for a movie. There's not a single theater in the Golan. But that's not what we're here for.

My mom checks the address and unfolds her pocket map of Haifa.

"We'll turn at Ha-Nevi'im Street," she says, pointing to the intersection three blocks away. "Then we take a left on Herzl. It's at the Hotel Zion, which should be down the street there."

The military is using a hotel ballroom for the photo identification center. We hurry down the sidewalk, past the movie theater, past the falafel shops and a small market.

Though it's a grand hotel with a fine-looking lobby, it's clear that the people milling around here are not on vacation. As we enter, I see that it's mostly women. There's a tight, pinched look to their faces. They're all here for the same reason we are.

"Excuse me," my mom asks one of them, "do you know where's the room with the photos?"

"Sure, I just came from there," she says. She's a young woman, her hair styled in a fashionable flip. Her expression is anything but cheerful. "I've been looking for my husband. He's a combat engineer."

"Did you find him?" my mom asks.

The woman shakes her head. "But it's a mess in there," she says. "There are thousands of photos. Some people are fighting over who's in a photo. It's a crazy way to do this." She shrugs and shakes her head, as if there was never a chance it would work out. But I can tell she's really disappointed.

My mom squeezes her hand in sympathy.

The woman points us to the right hallway. "I've heard there's another photo bank in Tel Aviv," she says. "It might have different photos. I'm going to try there next."

My mom and the other women we came with start debating whether it's worth hours on the bus to try the other photo bank if this one doesn't pan out.

"Good luck," I tell the woman.

"Thanks." She touches her stomach and sighs. Her face is pale and shiny with sweat.

"Are you okay?"

"I'm pregnant," she says. She looks down at her flat stomach and touches it again.

I blink in surprise.

"I wanted to wait to tell him until after Yom Kippur," she continues, as if I demanded to know more. "I thought it would be special to tell him after we broke the fast that, God willing, we would have a new name in the Book of Life. But while we were sitting in synagogue, a man walked in." Her voice takes on a dreamy tone, her expression far away. "I noticed right away that his shirt was sweaty under his arms, like he had been rushing around, which was strange on Yom Kippur. I didn't recognize him, which was also strange, because I know everyone in our neighborhood who comes to our synagogue. He carried a folder with him. That wasn't right either. He should have had a tallis bag and a prayer book. He headed straight to the bima and he interrupted the rabbi."

My mom and her friends have fallen silent, listening to the woman's story.

"The rabbi was so confused. He wasn't even angry with this stranger on the bima. I was in the front row of the women's balcony; I could see everything."

She falls silent again, lost in her memories. We have our story too. How the shelling came out of nowhere. How we fled in terror to the bomb shelters. How Dor was hurt, and how all our hard work in the fields burned up in a day. Everyone in our teeny, tiny country has their story, their moment when life changed on Yom Kippur. The lady's story makes me realize how small this country is, how we're all affected.

"What happened next?" I ask.

"The man was from the Defense Ministry. He was there to call all the reserve and active-duty soldiers to their bases immediately." She shivers. "That's when we knew something very bad was happening. We knew. It had to be war."

Goosebumps spread across my skin.

"He called name after name. And then the men got up to fight." She gives a helpless shrug. "We all knew what was waiting for them. We had just read the *Unetanneh Tokef.* We had been praying to be written into the Book of Life. Amit—my husband—looked up at the balcony when his name was called, looking for me. He blew me a kiss, and then he rushed out. I remember thinking that his white prayer shawl fluttered behind him like wings." She looks at me and gives me a sad sort of smile. "I rushed home to help him pack. He gave me a kiss, and then he left. I didn't have time to tell him our news. And now I'm waiting for him to fly back home to me." She touches her stomach again. "To us."

My mom's eyes well up, and she quickly dashes away tears. The two of them share a look, and something passes between them.

"Do you have a picture of him?" my mom asks. "We'll look again while we're in there. Here, I'll give you a photo of my son Motti. He's a tanker."

In such a small country, we look out for one another. And sometimes we find what we're looking for.

My mom reaches into her purse and pulls out a small black-and-white photo of Motti. She's already written his full name, rank, and unit on the back. We were planning to leave the photo with the soldier assigned to run the photo bank.

The woman rummages through her purse until she finds a spare photo of her husband. "This is Amit. I'm Bruria, by the way."

My mom introduces herself, the other women from the moshav, and me. We all look at the photo Bruria handed over.

Amit is a serious-looking man with thick, black-rimmed glasses. But there's something in his expression that seems to wink, like it's all one big joke and he's in on the punchline.

"What a handsome fellow," my mom says.

"He is," Bruria says, blinking quickly. "I know he's okay. I just know it."

We fall silent for a moment. We're thinking the same thing about Motti. All the people in this hotel poring over photos are thinking the same thing: Maybe their loved ones are alive. Maybe they will return home.

Bruria squares her shoulders and hurries off to catch the bus to Tel Aviv, her low-heeled shoes clicking as she makes her way through the lobby.

* * *

We enter a large room full of long tables, all of them covered in scattered issues of newspapers from around the world. Most are in Arabic, but there are some in English, French, Spanish—any paper that's published a photo of Israeli prisoners is here. Several televisions are playing loops of news reels that show Israeli prisoners sitting on the ground. Women huddle around the screens, squinting at the grainy video, groaning at every Israeli who doesn't look up when the camera passes by.

A uniformed soldier sits behind a desk with a ledger, writing down names as faces are recognized, making notes about rank and unit and age.

There are hundreds of newspapers; there are thousands of photos. There are duplicates and triplicates that only complicate the search.

I don't know what I was expecting, but the phrase *finding a needle in a haystack* bubbles up. How will we ever spot Motti in this mess?

My mom and the other women who came with us walk up to the tables and begin searching through the photos. I choose a table. The women on either side of me have been here a while. Their hands have turned black from touching all the newsprint.

I pick up a paper. There's a group shot— maybe a dozen men in the photo. Half of them are looking to the side or looking down. Parts of the photo are blurry. I squint, carefully eyeing each man. Motti? No, the chin is too pointy. Motti? No, the nose is too small. Motti? Maybe. But only the top of the head is visible. How is anyone supposed to know?

"Oh, my God!" someone cries. "Oh, dear Lord! It's Shmulic! I found him! He's here! Look! Look!" Other women crowd around a woman shouting and waving a newspaper.

The soldier sitting behind the desk looks up with interest.

As women crowd around her, someone takes

a closer look at the photo she's waving.

"That can't be Shmulic," she says. "That's my son! It's Chaim!"

"No," the first woman says, clutching the photo. "It's Shmulic."

"It's Chaim. I would know my son anywhere."

"You're saying I don't? Look at that face, the hair. It's Shmulic."

"Ladies, ladies, settle down, please," the soldier calls. "Bring the photo to me."

The crowd disperses as the two women, bodies stiff with anger, walk over to the soldier and show him the photo.

The three of them bend over the picture, voices quieter, trying to straighten out the confusion.

My mom looks up from her table, and we share a glance. How terrible. This whole thing. People just want a bit of proof that their loved ones are okay, and in their desperation, in their need for hope, they're turning on each other.

We spend a couple of hours in the ballroom, but we don't find Motti or recognize anyone we know. The faces start to blur. My fingertips turn gray, then black from the newsprint. The photos swirl together; all the faces look alike. I think I see Motti everywhere, only to discover it isn't him, again and again. I start to wonder if I even know what Motti looks like anymore.

A woman jostles me aside, grabbing the newspaper I was reaching for. She flips the pages aggressively, nearly ripping them as they turn. She's wearing a flowered housedress, the cheerful print at odds with the frantic look in her eyes. When she doesn't find what she's looking for, she throws the pages down on the table in a jumbled heap. She reaches for another edition, again nearly yanking it out of someone's hand. She's like a mother who's misplaced her toddler in a store, rushing from aisle to aisle, scanning high and low.

"Relax, okay?" another woman says. "These papers aren't going anywhere. You don't have to grab."

But it's as if the woman in the flowered dress doesn't even hear her. Again, she flips through the pages and throws the newspaper back on the table as she rushes to the next stack.

I rub my forehead. I have a headache.

My mom stops by my table. "Oy, look at you," she says, catching a glimpse of my face. She spits on a tissue from her pocket and rubs at my forehead.

"Ew, stop," I say, pushing her hand away.

Her hand drops to her side. She looks surprised at first but quickly shakes her head at herself. It's as if she forgot I'm twelve, not four.

"Run and get yourself some lunch, sweetie," my mom says, handing me a few liras. She looks drained, utterly exhausted. I am too.

"What about you?" I ask.

She waves away the question. "Don't worry about me; I'm fine. I want to look through some more tables before I take a break."

I step outside the hotel, eager to breathe in the fresh air. There's a faint hint of a salty breeze from the nearby Mediterranean. Out here, in the busy streets, the scene inside the ballroom seems like a bad dream. It's a normal day. I stretch my arms, arching my back, trying to ease some of the tension from hours of hunching forward, looking down at photos. My neck and back release with a series of quiet pops.

A few blocks away from the hotel, I find a small shawarma kiosk, where I order a pita full of hot savory meat and dripping, garlicky tahini sauce. My stomach rumbles with sudden hunger. The owner of the stand catches my eager smile as I take the sandwich and grins at me, showing a gold front tooth.

"Growing boys need to eat!" He scoops up a dozen cracked green olives swimming in brine and drops them into a twist of waxed paper. "A little extra, on the house."

Hanging behind him is a small blue tapestry with a fancy red border and Arabic writing embroidered in the center. He's an Israeli Arab, likely Muslim.

I accept the gift with thanks.

I eat the shawarma sitting under the shade of a giant bougainvillea, its bright purple flowers waving in the slight breeze. Two Hassidic women wearing long skirts, their hair covered by identical stiff brown wigs, walk by. An Arab woman wearing a long black abaya that covers her from head to toe passes them. She's carrying several plastic shopping bags bursting with food, probably returning from the same market the two Jewish women are walking to. Three businessmen in dark suits and ties pause to let the Arab woman skirt around them on the narrow sidewalk, then continue on their way, deep in conversation.

The woman from the lobby haunts me. Her story of the men rushing out of the service to go to war. I can picture it. Gideon did it. Motti did it. One day, I'll probably have to do it too.

Who are they? What are they like, the Syrians and the Egyptians who make war against us? Their newspapers look just like ours. Do they know that we like soccer and shawarma like they do? Would it matter if they knew that?

I eat the sour, salty olives and spit out the pits until the paper bag is empty. Finally I make myself leave my shady spot and return to the ballroom.

We don't find Motti's photo in the papers. My mom and I finally give up, fifteen minutes before the last bus to the Golan leaves.

My mom falls asleep on the ride back. Her head droops until it comes to rest on my shoulder.

She never did eat lunch. I sit very still, trying to give her a comfortable resting spot. We ride like that the rest of the way home. The green fields and the new trees and the migrating birds pass by the window and finally blur into nothing as I fall asleep too.

Chapter Thirteen

"Where were you yesterday?" Sara asks me. We're sitting together on the bus to school.

I tell her about the trip to Haifa to see the photos. "We didn't see Motti." I hesitate. "Didn't see Yuval, either."

She blinks. I can't read in her expression if she's relieved or not that I didn't see Yuval in a Syrian prisoner lineup.

"But there's another photo bank in Tel Aviv," I tell her. How strange that suddenly I'm hoping for confirmation that a loved one is a prisoner of war. That used to be one of the worst things I could imagine.

"I think Yuval's dead," Sara says bleakly.

A chill pierces my heart. "Why would you say

that?" It feels unlucky for her to speak her worst fear out loud. As if saying it will make it true.

"It's not official yet," she says. Tears shimmer on her eyelids, threatening to spill. "But one of Yuval's friends stopped by last night to tell us. His tank was hit. It caught fire." She pauses, her chin wobbling. "Sometimes there's no body. Then the army can't officially tell the families. But he said Yuval's tank was on fire. He saw it."

I think of Yuval with his mop of curly hair, his grin, and the gap in his teeth. Dead.

Sara's big brown eyes swim with tears behind her glasses. "You understand how I feel," she says. "You've lost a brother too."

She tucks her head against my shoulder. She's talking about Gideon, but I can't stop thinking of Motti. I cannot stand the fact that he's not here. He might never be. Like Gideon. And now Yuval. It's too much. I feel my composure start to crack.

Yoni and Ori, sitting across the aisle, look over. I feel the weight of their gaze. I'm about to cry on the bus. I'm bracing myself for their jokes, their disdain.

I feel the weight of a hand on my arm. "Beni," Yoni says, leaning over the aisle. His eyebrows are furrowed in concern. "What's wrong?"

"Sara got bad news about her brother," I say. I refuse to say that he's dead. I can't. "And we haven't heard anything from Motti. The fighting's been paused for two weeks now . . ." I can feel my chin start to tremble. It sounds so bad when I say it out loud. Motti would never stay silent for so long. He would have written, no matter how busy he was—something, even a one-line note, anything to let us know that he was okay, that he was alive. He would know how much we worry about him.

Ori looks away, staring at the floor in confusion and maybe even sorrow.

But Yoni is still leaning across the aisle. I wait for him to start making fun of me, of Sara. "Beni, I don't know what to say."

"There's nothing to say," I reply, almost angrily.

Yoni stays quiet for a moment. "Maybe Motti is okay," he offers.

"Yeah, sure," I say sarcastically. "Maybe."

I think of all the women in the hotel ballroom looking at those photos, everyone hoping for *maybe*.

I dash away the tears. I'm desperate to change the subject. Sara has turned away, pretending to be busy looking out the window.

"Did you review the chapter about Rome defeating Carthage yesterday?" I ask. Morah Yvette has been pushing forward with our history lessons about the Punic Wars, as if any of us care about a war from two thousand years ago. The funny thing is, so much of our history textbook is about war. Are schoolkids going to study us in two thousand years? Will they groan about trying to remember who was Egypt and who was Israel, why they fought, and who won?

"Yeah. There's going to be a test at the end of the week," Yoni says.

"Great," I say, rolling my eyes. "I haven't even started that chapter."

"Do you want to study together?" he offers.

I look over at Sara. We've already made plans, and I'm not about to ditch her.

"Sara and I were going to review it tomorrow," I say.

"Oh," Yoni says. He sits back in his seat. "Okay."

Sara finally turns away from the window. "You can come too," she says to Yoni quietly. She's pale, with salty tracks of tears on her cheeks. "We were going to study at my house after school."

"Really?" he says, smiling. "Okay, thanks."

"Can I come?" Ori asks uncertainly.

"Sure," Sara says with a tremulous smile. "We'll study together."

The rest of the ride to school is quiet, each of us lost in our thoughts. The bus descends from the Heights, and the wide spaces of the Golan slowly give way to the farms and fields of the Hula Valley. The air grows warmer. I wrestle open the window, and a breeze instantly blows inside.

A flock of storks standing in a marsh is startled by the bus passing them. They're so large that they look awkward as their long wings flap, working to get airborne. Just when it looks like nothing that heavy and clumsy could fly, they lift off, one after the other. They gain altitude with every flap, rising, then falling, then rising higher until it suddenly doesn't look hard anymore. The flapping wings grow more graceful, gliding away on an updraft until they are specks in the sky.

That's what living with grief is like. At first, almost too heavy to bear. Awkward and painful to see. Then slowly, slowly, it begins to be possible to live. Possible to feel happiness. But it's hard work to get there, and I'm tired.

I wish I could fly away with the storks. I wish the scariest thing in my life was a loud bus driving by.

I watch the storks until they vanish from sight, dissolving into the blue sky.

* * *

The next day after school the four of us disembark from the bus at Sara's moshav. Her moshav is similar to ours: small, modest homes identically built out of cinder blocks, with terracotta tile roofs.

The four of us walk along the road that runs through the moshav, passing the small synagogue and preschool, heading toward her house. Just like at our moshav, there's still a lot of damage from the war. We pass large divots left in the ground where mortars fell, damaged housing, and broken roofs covered with tarps to keep out the rain. The sounds of hammers and saws drone in the background as the construction continues. Ori goes on about something he heard about the test from an older student, raising his voice to be heard above the din.

We're almost at Sara's house when a military jeep passes us and pulls up to her front door.

Ori is oblivious, nattering on, but Sara lets out a strangled gasp. I feel the blood drain from my face. There's only one reason a military vehicle would come to her house. They're going to get an official notification about Yuval.

Sara reaches for my hand, and I grasp it. Yoni looks between us and back to the jeep, quickly understanding what's unfolding. Sadness and sympathy flash across his face.

Sara's hand is cold and clammy. Her breath whistles in and out.

The jeep comes to a stop, and a man hops out of the driver's-side door.

His uniform is filthy and stained. His skin is very dark, and he has wild, bushy hair and a thick beard. He jogs up the front path between the rows of flowers Sara's mom planted. At the front door, he doesn't even bother to knock. He just turns the handle and walks right in.

Sara and I freeze for a moment.

Even Ori finally realizes that something strange is going on. He falls silent mid-word, his mouth hanging open.

Sara drops my hand, and with a primal scream, she sprints to her house.

We can hear Sara's mom shrieking from inside the house, but instead of tears, instead of anguish, it sounds a lot like laughter, like joyful relief.

"Yuval!" Sara screams. "Yuval!"

Yoni, Ori, and I run after her.

The scene inside is not what I was expecting. Yuval is trying to keep his mom from hugging him.

"Ima, I'm filthy!" He dances out of her reach. "We need to burn this uniform. Don't touch it!"

But she doesn't care.

"I need to touch you," she says, crying and laughing at the same time. "I need to know you're real! They told us your tank was on fire. We thought you were dead!"

She chases him around the couch, arms out-stretched to hug him, as he skips and twists out of her reach.

"I'm disgusting," he cries. "I have lice!"

It's the strangest game of tag I've ever seen.

Sara stands by the front door, tears of happi-ness streaming down her face.

"Yuval," she says, her voice cracking. "We were so scared for you."

Yuval and their mom stop their chase. I can hardly recognize Yuval. Aside from the bushy hair and thick beard, the little visible skin on his face is nearly charcoal-black from soot, smoke, and dirt. It's clear that he hasn't showered since the war began. His uniform is no better: greasy, stained, and stiff with filth. Now that we're inside, I start to notice the smell too.

"Sara-leh, Ima," he says, "I'm okay." There's such emotion in his voice that it brings tears to my eyes. I look over at Yoni and Ori to find them just as moved. "I'm okay. But I really need a shower," he says. "I need to shave. And then I need to go straight back."

He reaches out and their mom grabs his filthy, dirt-stained hand. She presses it to her chest and then lifts it to imprint a kiss on it. Then she lets him go.

"I'll turn the hot water heater on," she says, "but after you're clean, you're not leaving without a meal."

"Ima—" he starts.

"No." She stops him. "I don't care what's going on there. It can wait for you to have a decent meal." After the silliness and the great joy, she's dead serious. There's a steely determination in her voice. "I'm not taking no for an answer."

Yuval sighs, some of the tension easing out of his shoulders.

"Okay, Ima," he says with a weary smile. "It'll be good to eat something that's not straight from a can." He presses a kiss to her forehead, careful not to touch her with anything other than his lips. "But quick, okay?"

She raises one eyebrow. "You want quick? Take your shower, and by the time you come out, I'll have a feast for you."

She puts the four of us to work. While Yuval scrubs off six weeks of grime and shaves a kilo's worth of hair, we chop and stir, set the table, and lay out a remarkable array of dishes at record speed. There's egg salad, tuna salad, chopped tomatoes and cucumbers, carrot salad, roasted eggplant, olives, hummus, an assortment of cheeses, and toast.

We've just put out a carafe of apple cider when Yuval emerges from the bathroom.

"This looks amazing," he says, rubbing his hands together. "You're the best."

He sits down and hungrily fills his plate to the brim.

"I wish I had known ahead of time that you were coming," his mother complains. "I would have made you a nice chicken. You need a hot meal."

He shakes his head, shoveling food into his

mouth as if he's never seen any before. "This is amazing," he says around a mouthful of pita and salad. "I haven't had anything fresh to eat in weeks."

He pauses. "Do we still have my old pair of eyeglasses?" he asks. In all the excitement, I didn't even notice that his glasses have a cracked lens.

For a moment, the happy atmosphere falters. It's a stark reminder that he's come from danger.

"I'm sure I can find them," his mom says, already rising from the table.

I suddenly realize that they only have these few moments together as a family, and that Yoni, Ori, and I should give them their space.

"Sara, we'll catch up tomorrow," I say. "Yuval, good luck out there."

"Great to see you, Beni," he says warmly, speaking around a towering forkful of egg salad. "Don't worry about a thing. Everything's fine."

I motion for Ori and Yoni to come with me. As we head for the front door, I hear Yuval.

"This salad is amazing! Did you make this, Sara?"

She replies happily as we walk out.

Yoni, Ori, and I walk back to our moshav, keeping to the gravel shoulder off the main road. Yoni and Ori talk over each other about how incredible it was to see Yuval. How gross he looked. How thrilled Sara was.

I'm happy for Sara. Really happy.

But horribly, selfishly, I can't stop thinking about Motti. Sara's family won the *maybe* lottery. And if they did, maybe we will too. Maybe Motti is just that busy. If there's no time for a shower or a shave or a normal meal, then maybe he really didn't have a second to jot down even one line on a postcard.

Maybe.

Or maybe they lucked out, and we won't.

I am tormented by the hope and the agony of *maybe*.

Yoni and Ori laugh and half-wrestle on the walk home, trying to trip each other. I pretend to join in, but my heart's not in it.

"How's Dor?" I ask Yoni. Even though we've been back at our moshav for a while now, I haven't seen the toddler. But a lot of the mothers are keeping their little kids close. After the sudden attack on Yom Kippur, it's a lot easier to believe there could be more surprises. No one wants their little ones far from the safety of the bomb shelters.

"He's fine," Yoni says dismissively.

"Can I come by and see him?"

My mom has also told me that Dor's doing fine. Now that he's been released from the hospital, no one except me seems to be worried about him. But there's a part of me that won't rest until I see him with my own eyes. I need some good news.

"Maybe some other time," Yoni says.

I kick a pebble in my way. "Is he really okay?" I ask after a moment.

"Sure, he's fine, but my mom's really weird about getting him excited. She's keeping him completely sheltered. It's like she wants to keep him in a jar on the shelf. Poor kid. She won't let him run around or do anything except nap and play with his toys."

Ori makes some kind of joke about kids in jars that Yoni finds hilarious. They're both in high spirits. I suggest a race, and we sprint the rest of the way home.

That night I tell my parents about Yuval.

I put a funny spin on it, making them laugh at Yuval dancing out of his mother's reach.

"He said, 'I have lice!'" I mimic the shimmy-shake he did to wiggle out of his mother's grasp.

"Oh God, lice," my mom groans. "You remember?" she asks my dad. "During the Independence War, everyone had them."

"Of course I remember," my dad said. "I had them everywhere." He turns to me and says in a conspiratorial voice, "There's a special kind that live on body hair. My underwear was crawling with them!"

"Gross!" I yelp. I hop up and down in my seat, feeling the phantom itch of invisible little critters.

"There was a water shortage," my mother explains, clearly feeling the need to defend my dad. "When people can't stay clean, the body lice move in."

"How do you get rid of them?" I ask, wide-eyed. I'm still imagining tickly little feet racing into every nook and cranny of my body.

"Kerosene," my dad says. "I rubbed it in

everywhere. Killed them all." There's plain relish in his voice. Even after all these years, his relief at being free of them feels fresh.

The advice about body lice quickly brings up other memories from my parents' past. The evening passes quickly as they share stories from their early days as pioneers: the food shortages, the wild optimism, the sense that anything was possible—including the creation of a new country, the only Jewish nation in two thousand years.

I go to bed that night willing myself to believe in the impossible.

Chapter Fourteen

Two days later, after a test on ancient Carthage and Rome, I'm returning from a trip to the bathroom when I overhear Morah Yvette and our principal, Noam, talking in the hallway.

"Are you sure I can't convince you to stay at least through the end of the school year?" he asks.

She takes a breath and rocks back on her heels, her hands clutching each other, as if for strength. "No." She shakes her head. "I need to return to France at the end of the semester."

I'm surprised by the sudden pang of loss. If someone told me at the start of the year that I would be sad for Yvette to leave, I would've thought that was nuts. But over the last few months, I've grown to like her. She's been trying her best, and she loves her students.

Yvette wrings her hands. "I didn't want to leave before the war ended, but things are looking much better now. I know it's okay to go. My family misses me very much. It's hard to be so far away. I have a little dog back home, too. It sounds funny, but he'll be glad to see me."

I slip back into class while they're still in the hallway and share the news with Sara.

"She's lonely," she whispers to me.

I lean over and whisper back, "We should introduce her to your uncle Mickey."

Sara looks at me, her eyebrows nearly touching the top of her head.

I nod for emphasis. "She'll love Goliath."

A slow smile spreads across Sara's face. I can't help but smile back. I can picture it. Mickey, unflappable, able to fix anything he can get his hands on. Yvette, missing her dog, looking for a home of her own in Israel. And Goliath, rolling on his back, letting her scratch his belly.

"We're having a big Shabbat dinner tomorrow," Sara whispers back. "I'll get my mom to invite her and Mickey. He can bring Goliath. My mom loves him."

"Perfect," I whisper. "Yvette and Mickey won't suspect anything."

"All right, everyone, settle down!" Morah Yvette shouts as she enters the room, once again fighting for control of the class. "We have a lot of work to do. One little war will not leave my students behind schedule."

On the ride home, Sara and I continue our plot.

I wish I could be there when Mickey and Yvette meet for the first time, but we agree it will seem more natural if it's just Sara's family and Yvette.

"You have to tell me all about it," I say, and Sara promises to do that.

* * *

Ori, Yoni, and I walk into our moshav together. I fill them in on Sara's plan for tomorrow.

"I don't think a Sabra mechanic will fall in love with a French teacher," Ori says doubtfully.

"You've never met Mickey," Yoni says. He turns to me, grinning. "I think it's a brilliant plan."

He claps me on the shoulder. Ori smiles hesitantly.

"You'd love Mickey," I tell Ori. "He was really patient when he taught us how to change oil in a car, and he's funny too."

"That's cool," he says, nodding and ducking his head. "It must be nice to know how to fix cars."

"Do you remember how he found the mice in that lady's car?" Yoni asks.

"Penina," I say, grinning at the memory.

"Yeah," Yoni laughs.

Ori looks between the two of us and looks down again. I fill him in on the story, laying on the details so he gets why it was funny. He laughs and shoots me a grateful look.

Yoni and Ori turn left toward their street while I continue straight toward my house.

I find both of my parents at home. They're sitting on the couch, a pitcher of lemonade with mint leaves on the low table in front of them. Lately, my dad has been coming home in the afternoon. He and my mom take a nap and then have a snack together before he heads back to his workshop.

"Thirsty?" my mom asks. "Come sit and tell me about your day."

"Morah Yvette says she's leaving," I tell her. "But Sara and I have a plan." I share our thoughts and watch my mom's face light up.

"Poor thing. It's not easy to be a new immigrant here. Falling in love with a local would certainly help." She's practically rubbing her hands together in glee. "But a boyfriend's not enough. She needs friends too. My friend Ruth's daughter is in her mid-twenties. Not married. They might get along. I'll call her tonight. I'll invite both of them for Shabbat next week so they can meet."

The lines of worry in that space between my mom's eyebrows ease as she gets busy with her plans. I sit back, smiling in satisfaction. With Yvette as my mom's new project, I suddenly feel confident that my teacher will change her mind about leaving before Hanukkah. We're discussing other possible people to introduce to Yvette when there's a firm, confident knock on the door.

"Who could that be?" my mom muses. "Are you expecting someone?" she asks my dad.

"What?" he asks, looking up from the paper he's engrossed in.

As she gets up to open the door, my mom half-turns back to me. "Gallit!" she says. "That's another possibility. She just moved to Merom Golan. That's not far from here. She works in the preschool there. And her mother was from Belgium, so she speaks some French."

She opens the door and freezes.

There are two soldiers in dress uniform at our door.

For a moment, there's utter silence. I'm nailed to my seat in shock, unable to move. My mom's back is to me. She is so still, it's like she's been turned to wood. We are a frozen tableau, our edges as thin as a soap bubble. Our *maybe* is about to pop.

"Is he dead?" my mom asks in a low, choked voice. Her nightmare encapsulated in three words.

My father drops the paper and gets to his feet so quickly that he knocks over his glass of lemonade. The sticky juice spills everywhere. He doesn't even glance at it. His hands are clenched in fists by his sides. I can see his pulse flutter in the hollow of his neck.

I suddenly wish for *maybe* to come back. I can live with *maybe*. I want Motti to be okay, and *maybe* means he might be. I want to keep pretending that Motti is too busy to write us. But now that the soldiers are here, I can't pretend anymore.

My mother is trembling as if she's freezing. She knows the soldiers are here to tell us nothing good. But unlike me, she wants to know.

"May we come in?" the soldier asks. He's not young—a career officer in his mid-thirties. His hair is bushy, and he's overdue for a shave; a dark stubble covers the lower half of his face. The other soldier is younger, though still older than Motti. They both look tired, their eyes puffy with lack of sleep.

"Just tell me," my mom says roughly. "Tell me right now. Is Motti dead?"

I clench my fists and hold my breath, waiting for their answer.

"No," says the younger one. He leans a little around the first one. "We don't think he's dead."

My mom sags slightly, leaning against the door frame.

I'm dizzy with relief. Motti's not dead? My heart starts to soar and sing. This is better than *maybe*. This is good news!

"Motti's alive?" I cry. I grab my father's hand, wanting to cry and scream with joy. "Abba, it's okay," I say. He has a strange look on his face. "Motti's alive! It's okay." My dad places a hand on my shoulder, squeezing lightly.

It takes me a moment to realize that no one else in the room is excited. My mom is still leaning against the door for support. She turns to look at my dad, and I see a mix of hope and anguish on her face.

"May we come in?" the officer asks again.

My mom steps aside and the two men enter.

"What's going on?" I'm living in a nightmare where nothing makes sense. Why aren't my parents relieved? Why aren't we all celebrating?

"It appears that your son has been captured

by the Egyptians," the officer says, taking a seat. "We believe he is a prisoner of war."

My mom's still standing. She wraps her arms around her middle and gazes at the floor, rocking back and forth. My dad sinks down to the couch, looking sick.

With both my parents overcome, I fire question after question. When was Motti captured? Was he injured? How many other POWs are with him? Where is he being held? What is the government doing to get him released? Can we send him a care package? Can he write to us? Can we send him a letter? Why did they take so long to tell us?

The questions fly out faster than either soldier can answer. My mom, in a moment of bizarre habit, walks over to the table, pours two glasses of lemonade, and presses them into the soldiers' hands, as if to turn them into guests.

"There's still a lot we don't know," the soldier says, raising his hands to stop my interrogation. He looks in surprise at the glass in his hand, takes a sip, and sets it down. "The Egyptians haven't released a list of the names of all their prisoners. But your son's photo was published in an Algerian newspaper, and someone in Tel Aviv recognized it."

He reaches into his pocket, pulls out a folded newspaper sheet, and carefully unfolds it. It's similar to the dozens and dozens of papers my mom and I pored over in Haifa, but we never saw this one.

My parents and I huddle over it.

It's a close-up of three soldiers sitting on the ground with their hands laced and resting on top of their heads. Motti is the one on the right. He's unmistakable.

My mom lets out a strangled sound.

Motti looks serious but calm. He isn't as dirty and unkempt as Yuval was, which makes me wonder if he was captured early on in the war. During all these weeks when we were hoping for a postcard, has he been sitting in an Egyptian prison?

My mom grabs for the photo, clutching it in both hands. She sits down heavily next to my dad, as if her legs have given out.

"Before we go any further, can you confirm

this is your son?" the soldier asks. "Is this Mordechai Laor?"

My mom has tears streaming down her face. She touches the image lightly, as if Motti can feel her touch.

My dad puts his arm around my mom's shoulder.

The soldiers are still waiting for my parents to answer, but for a moment, they seem struck silent.

"Yes," I say, speaking for all of us. "That's Motti."

"You bring him back," my dad says to the soldiers. His voice quavers for a moment. He swallows, breathing heavily through his nose. "You hear me? You bring him back. I don't care what it costs."

"The prime minister is doing everything she can. Getting our troops home is her highest priority," the officer says. He keeps talking— explaining the situation, the variables, the unknowns, urging us to be patient and to have confidence—but I've stopped listening.

My hands curl into fists. My fingernails dig

into my palms. My heart pounds in my chest as my dad's words ricochet in my mind like bullets.

You bring him back.

My dad was commanding the soldiers, but it feels like he charged me with this task. I'm the last son he has left, the baby of the family. The one Motti always has to defend. And now Motti is captured. He needs someone to rescue *him*. I hear my dad's words.

Bring him back.

The soldiers and my parents continue to talk, working through our new reality, explaining how the military and the government are doing everything they can. My parents sit together, leaning close to listen, but I get up and walk to my room. My heart is racing, pounding in my chest. I lie in my bed, glaring at the ceiling.

I'm so sick of feeling helpless. Gideon. Dor. Yuval. And now Motti. Yuval ended up fine. But for Motti, it's back to being a *maybe*.

I can't accept this.

I won't.

Chapter Fifteen

In the days that follow, my parents and I live in a sort of dream-like world. My dad goes to work. My mom goes to the grocery store and cooks and cleans. I go to school. We look a lot like a normal family living a normal life. But we're like ducks: calm and steady on the surface, while underwater, we're frantically paddling to stay afloat. It takes concentration to go about my daily life. I feel like I'm split in two. One part of me takes notes in class and cares about my grade on the Punic Wars test. The other part can't remember why school matters. The only thing that matters is Motti.

I eat lunch alone, sitting on the ground under an oak tree at the edge of the schoolyard. It's a cold day. The breeze carries smells of plowed dirt and traces of diesel exhaust from the tractor working on a nearby farm. When I finish eating my apple, I fling the core as hard as I can. It goes soaring over the fence that surrounds the schoolyard and plops into a thicket of bushes. A part of me wonders if, ten years from now, there will be an apple tree growing just out of reach of the students at this school. Kids will wonder who would be cruel enough to plant an apple tree so close, yet impossible for them to reach.

"Mickey and Yvette went out to dinner last night." Sara plops down on the grassy spot next to me and opens her lunch sack. Her cheeks and nose are pink from the cold air. "My mom says she's never seen Mickey so excited about meeting someone."

The other kids at school all know about Motti by now. I can feel them watching me—uncertain what to say, what to do. Sara's approach is to pretend everything is fine. I try to play along.

"That's great," says the part of me that cares about anything that doesn't deal with Motti. "I'm happy for them."

I guess I'm not as convincing as I thought, because Sara gives me an anxious look.

"I don't mean—I just—" She stumbles for words. "Beni, I have a really good feeling about this."

"Sure," I say dully. "They're perfect for each other."

"I don't mean Yvette and Mickey. I mean everything. Motti's going to come back. You'll see. It's going to be fine."

But it doesn't always turn out fine. Sometimes older brothers don't come back. I hate this feeling of waiting to see how it all turns out. I want to go to Golda Meir and say, *He's my only living brother! What are you waiting for? Stop wasting time. Make the Egyptians bring him back!*

I want to yell at Sara: *Don't you realize how lucky you are? Just because your brother is fine doesn't mean mine will be.*

It takes effort to bite back the words. I turn my head away from her, fighting for composure. After a moment, Sara takes the hint and leaves me alone.

My parents are living in their different *maybe* dream worlds. Halfway through preparing a recipe, my mom looks in confusion at the mess in the bowl. "Did I add the baking power?" she asks out loud. Even when she doesn't forget an ingredient or add it in twice, her cookies and cakes come out all wrong.

The chicken at dinner is sour. The salad is sweet. The bread is stale and crumbly. But it doesn't matter because none of us has any appetite anyway. We scrape the uneaten food off our plates straight into the trash. My mom frowns at the waste but doesn't have the energy to scold us.

My dad, in the meantime, is angry. He walks through his day in a constant state of shimmering temper that explodes at the slightest provocation. He yells at the mail carrier for crumpled letters. He scolds the attendant at the gas station for a messy countertop. He is not like my usual, easygoing dad who laughs off people's eccentricities. Nothing is funny anymore.

We need Motti back. We're falling apart without him.

I read every news article about the Egyptians, trying to understand their thinking, trying to guess what they might do to the Israelis under their control.

What is Motti doing right now?

Is he hungry? Is he cold? Is he in pain?

We leave care packages and letters with a Red Cross representative who will try to get them to Motti.

Life continues without us.

Back in class after lunch, Yvette hands out the tests we took last week. I missed nine questions. Yvette calls me to her desk. Quietly, so the other students won't hear, she offers to let me retake the test next month.

"Take some time," she says. "Study the material. You're a bright student; I know you can do better. This isn't like you."

I cannot stand the pity I see in her eyes. "No, thank you," I say.

"Think about it," she urges. "It's a big part of your grade."

"It doesn't matter."

She opens her mouth to argue with me, but

she closes it again quickly. She exhales. "How about we talk about this in a few weeks? You might feel differently."

I shrug a shoulder.

Two weeks pass with no news.

I think about the Egyptians daily. I hate them. I wish God would send down ten new plagues to torment them. Hail. Locusts. Darkness. *Let my brother go.*

On the other hand, Israel holds several thousand Egyptian prisoners. They are Motti's ticket home. A prisoner exchange is the only way to get Motti back. I find myself in the strange position of hating the Egyptians who are in Egypt and praying for the safety and well-being of the ones in Israel.

My dad drives to Nafah each day, hanging around, trying to get news. But the commander there doesn't know how progress on an exchange is going. My dad's anger with the world grows.

Rumors swirl. Someone has heard there's going to be an exchange next week. Someone says there's already been a small swap. Someone says the Russians are blocking the exchange to get back at our American allies. Someone else says the Americans might not support an exchange unless we agree to release the Egyptian Third Army in the Sinai.

Every new rumor ratchets up the tension in my house.

My mom scrubs every surface, as if she can clean her way out of this mess. I come to hate the smell of bleach.

"Don't walk through here with your shoes on!" she yells at me when I come home. "You're leaving tracks. Go play outside!"

"It's raining," I protest. It's a dreary day. The dark gray clouds and the cold rain outside match my mood inside. But that doesn't mean I want to spend time immersed in this weather.

"I just spent two hours cleaning the floor," my mom huffs.

"But—"

"Your father is going to Nafah again. Go with him. By the time you come back, the floor will be dry." I'm standing in the doorway, banned from my own house. "You'd better leave your shoes outside when you get back!" she warns, her voice tight and shrill—nothing like her usual calm, confident tone. "Don't come back here tracking muddy footprints!"

I turn and go back into the chilly rain. The moshav looks empty and abandoned in this bleak weather. Piles of debris from the broken houses, chunks of asphalt, and twisted metal have yet to be cleared.

I run down the street to my dad's carpentry shop, shoulders hunched against the cold and the dampness. I pass houses with plastic sheeting pinned to their roofs, covering holes that have yet to be repaired. The craters in their yards from the shelling are filled with muddy water. There's no one outside but me.

My thoughts turn to Motti. Is he cold in Egypt? Is he alone? Now that it's winter, has he been given a sweater? A blanket? I've grown used to thinking of these questions, knowing I can't get answers. But I can't stop myself from fretting. I shiver from more than just the cold.

I find my dad staring blankly out the window, his back to the door. Raindrops slip and slide down the cracked glass pane. Several half-finished projects sit on his work table. But his tools lie unused, and his clever hands—hands that can fix anything they touch—hang still by his side.

"Abba," I say.

He starts and turns. "Beni, is everything okay?"

"It's fine. Ima sent me to come with you to Nafah."

A bit of tension slumps from his body. We're all on high alert, braced for news to come at any moment, good or bad.

"That'll be nice. I'll be glad for the company," he says with a smile. It's a shadow of his usual grin.

As we drive together to the military base, the snick and click of the windshield wipers are the only sounds in the car. The security guard at the gate recognizes my dad and waves us through without looking at my dad's identification.

My dad parks in front of a nondescript beige building. We step out of the car, hopping around the giant puddles. Unlike at our moshav, lots of people are outside on base, rushing from one building to another. There's a hum of activity in the air. Since the ceasefire in October, the war has been paused, but it's far from over. Everyone is still on heightened alert. Even on a cold, rainy day, there's lots to do.

My dad holds the door open for me, and we both hurry inside the commander's office suite.

A space heater is working overtime. The small outer reception area is stuffy and smells like wet wool with traces of smoke.

The secretary's desk is piled high with memos and letters. There's a sheet of paper threaded through her typewriter. She's on the phone, the plastic beige receiver tucked between her ear and her shoulder as she writes down a message for the commander.

Her eyes widen when she sees us. I feel my dad tense next to me.

"Good, good. Got it," she says to the caller and waves for us to go past her desk to the commander's door. She covers the mouthpiece of the phone. "We were just about to send someone to see you," she whispers. "We have news. Good news."

My dad and I exchange looks. My heart speeds up. Good news.

"Is there a letter from him?" I ask her. I don't want to hope for too much. Frankly, even thinking there's a letter feels like hoping for too much. It might be something as small as direct talks starting or Russia offering to facilitate discussions.

She doesn't answer, already back to listening to the person on the line and writing down a message.

I square my shoulders and tell myself to be happy with whatever the news is, however small, as long as it's good news. I glance at my dad. His whole face is lit with excitement. He's expecting something big. I worry about what's going to happen when he's disappointed.

My dad knocks briskly. The commander shouts, "Come in!" and we enter.

His office is lined with topographical maps of the Golan. There are dune-colored filing cabinets and a large desk covered in files and reports.

The commander, a slim man with thinning hair, leaps to his feet when he sees us. "We have an agreement!" he declares, his lined face breaking out in a wide smile.

"I knew it!" my dad crows. "I just knew!"

"What?" I say. "What's going on?"

"Is this your son?" the commander asks my dad. He doesn't wait for an answer. He comes around the desk to clap each of us on the shoulder. "We reached an agreement with the Egyptians. Starting in four days, we're going to exchange prisoners: 8,400 Egyptians for 238 Israelis." I stare at him in shock. He shakes me a little, as if to wake me up. "I told you," he says to my dad, "Golda was going to bring back our boys. She wasn't going to sleep until they were all back."

The commander grips my dad by the back of his neck. The tendons on either side are strained. "You're going to see Motti in less than a week."

My dad looks away, blinking rapidly. I'm trembling, shaking with the news. It's everything I dreamed of, but at the same time, I almost can't believe it.

The men embrace. My dad pulls me in, and I'm almost crushed between them. The smells of sweat, machine oil, and laundry soap fill my nose.

The commander clears his throat with emotion. "It's going to be okay," he says to us.

"Can we trust them?" I ask roughly. It kills me to ask this, to doubt this good news. But I have to know.

"There are no guarantees," the commander says bluntly. "But the Russians and the Americans want this. The Egyptians aren't going to blow this up. It's good for them too, believe me. We're going to be fine."

"How is it going to work?" I ask. "How does an exchange happen?"

"We're going to drive the Egyptians in buses to the border," he says. "On the other side, they're letting the Red Cross fly our men out. The first men to come home are the injured ones. I can tell you, Motti's name is not on that list. So that's great news too."

"Oh. Good." It *is* good that he's not on the injured list, of course, but at the same time, I just want him back. Now. Before anything changes.

"We give them their injured first as well.

After that, we start loading them and sending them off in batches. The whole thing will take days. You'll have to be patient; we won't know who's on the plane until the pilot calls in the manifest. They'll land at Lod. We're recommending that everyone just stay home. Believe me, we will call you with any news we get."

"We'll wait at the airport, then," my dad says firmly.

"Yoram," the commander says, "I hear you. I'd feel the same way if it were my son. But please, listen to me. Wait for us to call you. There's no point in causing a mad scene at the airport. There are hundreds of families in your position. It's going to take days to get all our boys home. If all the families camp out at the airport day after day, it will be bedlam. Give our boys a second to breathe, to get their boots back on Israeli soil, before the world crashes on them."

"That makes sense," my dad says. "Absolutely."

"So you'll wait for us to call?"

My dad makes a sort of shake-and-nod head waggle motion. "Sure," he says.

We can all tell there's no way he's not going to be at the airport. Every day, all night, whatever it takes.

"Okay, glad you're hearing me," the commander says, wryly. "We'll keep you posted."

"Where are the Egyptians being held?" I ask. "Where are the buses leaving from?"

"Atlit," he says.

Atlit is just south of Haifa, about two hours from here. There's a detainee camp there from the time of the British Mandate, before Israel was a country. Our frugal nation uses a camp built by the British to hold Jews twenty-five years ago to hold Arab prisoners today. I try to imagine what they look like, what their life in the prison is like. Do they have enough to eat? Do they have books to read or something to do? Do their families know they're safe?

The phone is ringing again, and the secretary walks in with half a dozen messages. The commander clasps my dad in a quick hug and returns to his desk.

"It's good news, Yoram," he repeats as he picks up the phone. "It's what we've been waiting for."

We hurry back into the cold rain. It doesn't seem nearly as dreary anymore. Rain brings life, after all. The ground drinks it; the trees and animals need it. We need it too. Rain is the promise of life, and after the commander's news, we have a promise of life too.

"I can't wait to tell Ima," I say. "The look on her face . . ."

We exchange a quick grin.

"I knew they were looking out for our boys," my dad says with satisfaction.

"I can't believe we're actually going to see Motti next week!" I say, bouncing a bit in my seat.

"Slow down. It's not a done deal yet, Beni," my dad warns. "We have to be braced for delays or changes. Until we have him home, it's not over."

I shiver at his words, my happiness suddenly dulled. I stay mostly silent on the short ride back to our moshav. I can't stop thinking about the Egyptians. I didn't realize they were just two hours away from us. I had thought they were being held in the south, close to the border.

"Abba," I say as sudden inspiration strikes

me, "we aren't far from Atlit. We could go! We could go right now."

"Why would we do that?" my dad asks, looking at me in confusion.

"To see the Egyptians, to make sure they're okay. To make sure everything is ready to go, so that there aren't any delays."

It's so obvious to me. We can't control what happens with the Israeli prisoners in Egypt, but at least we can make sure everything's right on our end.

"Beni," my dad says. He looks like he wants to laugh. "It's a military base. They're not going to let us in."

"They let us in Nafah all the time."

"That's different; they know us here. And besides, there's nothing we could do to help in Atlit. We would only be in the way. No, no." He shakes his head as I try to argue my case. His hands are firmly at the wheel, driving us back to our house. "The best thing is to let the experts do what they need to do. They're doing a great job so far. They're bringing our boys home." His voice rises in his joy.

My dad talks and talks. His anger has drained away, and his normal cheerfulness has come roaring back. He doesn't seem to mind that we still have unknowns in front of us.

His voice fades into the background as my thoughts churn. The more I think about it, the more it sinks in that Motti's safe return depends on the Egyptian prisoners' safe return to Egypt. Forget waiting at the airport for Motti to arrive. Someone needs to go and keep an eye on the Egyptians. To make sure that nothing happens to them. They *have* to get back to Egypt. If anything goes wrong with that, the whole deal will collapse.

Chapter Sixteen

Three days later, my parents tell me to expect them to be home late.

"The military set up a meeting with a counselor," my mom says. "She's going to advise the families on how we can help our boys get used to normal life again."

"What does that mean?" I ask. "We're his family. Motti's going to be happy to be home. That's not complicated."

"That's true," my mom agrees. She's wiping down the kitchen table as I put the milk from our breakfast back into the refrigerator. "But it's a big psychological strain to be a prisoner of war. And the military has learned some things that can make healing from that easier."

"It's not going to be a problem for Motti," I predict. It takes me a moment to find a spot for the milk. The fridge is surprisingly full.

"I agree, but it doesn't hurt to listen," my mom says. "I've left schnitzel for you in the fridge; go ahead and eat dinner without us. We probably won't be home until eight, maybe later."

I freeze for a moment.

My mom notices. "You're not worried about being home alone after dark, are you?" I used to be afraid of the dark, but I've long since learned that bad things are just as likely to happen in the daylight. It's been years since I slept with a nightlight.

"Ima." I roll my eyes. "No, of course not. I'm twelve." My mind races with the sudden opportunity. "Take your time. I'll be fine."

"You're a sweet boy," my mom says, ruffling my hair, and I give her an angelic smile.

She has no idea that instead of going to school, I've decided to go to Atlit.

I know what my dad said, but *what if*? What if the people in charge do need help with something? What if they're doing something wrong?

I need to see it for myself. Motti has to come home.

I've looked up the bus schedule. I have money for the fare. I can take the same bus I take to school at Kibbutz Lavi and from there grab a bus to Haifa. From Haifa, I can catch a commuter bus to Atlit. The whole trip should take about three hours, which leaves me a couple of hours to try to check on the Egyptians before I catch the bus in time to get home by dinner.

I've been wondering how I could be away without my parents worrying, but now that they'll be gone until eight, I have the whole day to get there and back. It's a perfect plan.

Except for one thing.

* * *

"Where are you going?" Sara asks me.

We sat on the bus to Kibbutz Lavi together, like we always do. But when she turns to walk to our school, I stay at the bus stop outside the kibbutz, waiting for the bus to Haifa.

"I have things to do today," I say mysteriously.

Sara is unimpressed. "Like what?"

"What are you guys waiting for?" Yoni calls. "We're going to be late."

"Just go," I call back. "I have something to do today."

"You're skipping school?" Yoni asks, trotting back to us. "I'm in!"

"No! You're not invited." This isn't going according to plan.

Ori walks over to us as well. "What's going on? Why are you all standing here?"

I don't have time to explain. The bus to Haifa is coming down the road. I fumble in my pocket for my money.

The bus slows down and comes to a stop in front of us. The sweet smell of diesel from the idling motor fills the air. The bus doors open with a swoosh, and three ladies climb down.

"I'll see you guys later," I say as I board the bus.

Sara, Yoni, and Ori gape at me.

"Where are you going?" Sara asks in confusion.

I pull my money out and hand it to the driver.

"I'm going to help Motti get home," I tell my friends over my shoulder.

The driver takes my money, punches a ticket, and hands it to me. The door whooshes closed behind me.

I take a free window seat and see the three of them looking at me with identical bewildered expressions. I wave as the bus pulls away from the curb. They grow smaller and smaller behind me.

* * *

I'm excited and queasy at the same time. It was easy to act nonchalant in front of Ori, Yoni, and Sara, but now that I'm on the bus, some big doubts have cropped up. What if I get lost? How will I get into the base? What will I do once I get in? What if this is a terrible idea? My stomach starts to cramp with nerves. To distract myself, I try to plan my strategy.

I come up with a cover story about how my brother is a prison guard at the base and I'm coming to visit him for lunch. If I play it right, I'll be able to trick the gate guard into letting me in. I practice my lines over and over in my head.

Once I'm in, I'll make sure everything happening with the exchange looks okay, and then I'll head straight back home.

* * *

The first part of my plan goes off without a hitch.

I disembark at the bustling central bus station in Haifa and find the commuter bus to Atlit. I arrive at Atlit before lunch. It's noticeably warmer here than on the Golan Heights. The late-autumn sun is hot on my skin, baking the sidewalk and heating the air around me. There's sand on the side of the road.

On either side of me are cotton fields. They've been recently harvested, and a few wisps of white cotton still cling to the brown, dried-out stalks.

Three other people disembark with me—workers coming in for their shift at the prison.

They hurry off, casting curious looks in my direction.

The first thing I see are the watchtowers. There are armed guards in each one, and several of the towers even have mounted machine guns. The whole perimeter is fenced and topped with barbed wire. Through the chain links, I see dozens of low-slung barracks, and behind them, rows and rows of canvas tents, hastily put up to accommodate the thousands of prisoners who are past the capacity of the prison.

There's a security gate with large doors for vehicles and a smaller gate for individuals. The people who disembarked from the bus with me show their IDs, sign in, and walk through. It's my turn now. How I handle this will determine whether I get to see the Egyptians or not. I wish I had Motti's easy confidence. He can make anyone agree to anything he wants.

"I'm here to visit my brother," I tell the guard.

"Who's your brother?" he asks. The guard's a young guy, probably not much older than Motti. He looks tired and bored. He has thick, hairy eyebrows, and pimples dot his cheeks like red freckles.

"Motti," I say automatically.

And here, less than a minute into my big plan, I run into trouble.

"Motti?" he asks in confusion. "Motti who?"

Motti is a common Israeli name. I assumed there would be a Motti working on the base.

"Um, he works with the Egyptians here," I say. I can hear the nervousness in my own voice.

"Huh?" The guard looks at me with a mix of puzzlement and impatience.

"I'm bringing him lunch." I lift my school lunch pail as proof.

He shakes his head. "Buddy, I don't know what you're playing at. This is a military prison, not a picnic site. You need to go."

"No! Please! Let me in." My plan is in shambles. Nothing's working like I hoped it would.

"No!" The guard loses his patience. "Get out of here."

"I came all the way from the Golan," I say, deciding I'd better just tell the truth. "I have to see the Egyptians."

"This isn't a zoo, kid," he says. "Go back to school."

I feel tears of frustration well up. "I know it's not a zoo," I say hotly. "I just want to see them." I search for a way to explain my obsession with them. The way I stay up at night, thinking about what Egypt is like, why they hate us, what Motti's life is like there. "My brother's been in Egypt for six weeks. His name is Motti Laor. He's a tanker, and he's a prisoner there. I just . . . I want to be sure the Egyptian prisoners are okay, because then my brother will be okay."

I run out of words. What am I doing here? It made sense to come here this morning, but now that I'm here, my reasoning sounds ridiculous.

The guard sighs.

"I'm sorry." He shakes his head. "I feel for you. But I can't let you in here."

How can I tell him I'm here to make sure nothing goes wrong with the exchange? I'm twelve. It's absurd.

"Please?" I try again. "I won't make any trouble. I won't stay long."

"I can't let you in. I just can't." He leans close and lowers his voice. "I shouldn't tell you this, but . . ." He pauses and looks over his shoulder. "The first group of Egyptians will bus out today. Nothing can go wrong. If the Egyptians think we're not holding up our end of the bargain, not just the prisoner exchange but the whole cease-fire might fall through. You understand?"

I nod. Of course. That's why I'm here. Nothing can go wrong with the exchange. My parents and I are nervous about trusting the Egyptians. The Egyptians must feel the same about us.

"So the last thing—the very last thing—we need is to have anything weird happen that throws us off schedule. They have to be at the border on time. I have to do my part here and keep things strictly by the rules."

He really does look sorry. I think quickly, trying to salvage the situation as best I can.

"Can I stay here until the bus comes by?" I ask. Even seeing the Egyptians pass by in the bus could be worthwhile. Seeing them headed back, knowing the exchange is starting, would be wonderful.

The guard looks uncomfortable. Clearly, he'd rather I just go away.

"I'm really sorry. But you can't stay here. There're people coming and going, and it's not right to have a kid lingering nearby. I'll get in trouble. I don't want anything to go wrong here."

I try to think of what I could do to convince him to let me stay, to let me in, but nothing comes. This is something that Motti would be able to do. He could talk his way into a bank safe if he wanted to.

But it's as clear as it's ever been: I'm not Motti.

"I'm serious," the guard says. The sympathy in his voice drains away. I'm a nuisance, a problem to remove. "You need to go."

My shoulders slump as I realize this whole trip has been for nothing. I've used up all my savings to pay for the round-trip bus fare, and for what? The crushing disappointment wrestles with my huge feelings of stupidity. What was I thinking? I stand on my tiptoes, hoping to get a glimpse at the base behind him.

"Haven't you heard anything I've said? You need to go now!" the guard scolds.

"Okay," I say. "I'm going."

I turn and walk back to the bus stop, feeling his gaze on me the whole time.

There's no bench, so I take a seat on the scalding hot sand. Insects buzz by me as I wait for the next bus to Haifa. What a stupid day. I smack my arm and squish a mosquito. It's such a letdown.

I'm still waiting for the bus to arrive when the main gates of the base swing open. Jeeps with mounted machine guns drive out. Behind them are two buses and behind *them*, two more jeeps.

I scramble to my feet as the convoy passes. My heart knocks in my chest. My low mood swings up so fast that I want to jump and cheer. This is it. The prisoner exchange has begun.

I try to catch a glimpse of the Egyptians in the bus windows, but they pass by too quickly for me to get more than a fuzzy impression of dark-haired men.

A plume of exhaust in their wake makes the air shimmer.

After a while, I sit back down on the sand. At least I saw them, I tell myself. I actually saw the convoy heading to the border. Are Israelis being taken to the airfield to be sent home too? Maybe. My heart squeezes with hope. *Maybe.*

After what feels like forever, a city bus finally arrives. It's got a different route number than the one I took to get here from Haifa.

"Does this bus go to Haifa?" I ask the driver when I board.

He sucks on his teeth and moves around a mouthful of sunflower seed shells that he spits into a paper bag.

"Eventually," he says. "This route goes into Atlit, then south, and then back around to Haifa."

What he's describing will add at least an hour to my travel time.

"When does the next bus to Haifa come here?" I ask.

"Not till five," he says.

"What?" I say in shock.

"Yep," he says, popping more sunflower seeds into his mouth. "Don't like it? File a complaint with the prime minister. Now are you coming on or not?"

I sigh. "Yes." Waiting until five to catch a bus to Haifa is not really an option.

I find a seat toward the front and lean my head on the glass. The windows are down, and once the bus starts moving, a breeze flutters my hair and my shirt, drying the sweat that pooled while I waited.

We stop and let off passengers in Atlit before rolling onward again.

About half an hour later, we're on a stretch of quiet road between towns when the driver slows to get a look at the commotion on the side of the road. Two military buses have pulled over, and military jeeps have parked on either side of them.

As my bus passes them, I get a quick glimpse of one of the buses with its hood up. Several soldiers mill around it, hands on hips, peering inside.

It's the prisoner exchange convoy.

"STOP!" I shout, leaping to my feet. "Stop the bus!"

Instinctively, the driver slams the brakes, and I almost go flying forward. I grab at the seatback in front of me and barely stop myself from tumbling over it.

"What's wrong?" the driver says. Passengers in the back call out in annoyance.

"I need to get off!"

"This isn't a stop, kid," he says. "There's nothing here."

"Don't you see them?" I gesture behind me to the convoy stopped on the side of the road. "They need help!"

He shakes his head. "The military? Breaking down is normal." He shrugs. "When I served back in '52, we didn't have a week without some kind of breakdown on the side of the road. They've got it covered."

"No, you don't understand. Those are Egyptians on those buses. This is the prisoner exchange!"

At the mention of Egyptians, he sits up and looks behind him. A few passengers who overhear our conversation peer out the window.

"How do you even know that?" he asks.

"That doesn't matter now," I say impatiently. "We have to see if there's something we can do to help." The clock's ticking. The prisoners have to get to Egypt on time.

He lets out a huge sigh. "You scared me, son. But I have a job to do, and that's getting this bus to the next stop."

"I'm getting off," I say. "Someone needs to help them."

"Nu!" someone shouts from the back of the bus. "Why are we stopping? I'm going to be late to my appointment."

A sudden idea occurs to me.

"Hey, maybe you can give them your bus. You know, swap and then wait with the broken one until someone can come fix it."

"My bus!" the driver says, rearing back in horror. "I'm not giving anyone my bus."

"You don't understand how serious this is!" I shout, losing my patience. I head to the door. "Just let me off then."

"How are you going to help them?" he says in irritation. "They need a mechanic."

"Just let him off already," someone says.

"I need to get to my appointment."

Muttering under his breath, the bus driver opens the door. I hurry down the steps before he can change his mind. As soon as I'm off, the door shuts behind me, and the bus pulls away.

Half a dozen people are standing around the side of the road, and about fifty men are sitting cross-legged on the ground. The Israeli soldiers are wearing green khaki uniforms. The people sitting on the ground are wearing identical pale jumpsuits. They're the Egyptian prisoners. I stop to gawk, but a soldier—chubby with a round face and a small button nose—grabs me by the arm.

"What are you doing here?" he asks. "This is no place for children."

There's a captain off to the side, screaming into a short-distance radio with a huge antenna sticking out of it.

"We need the mechanic now—right now. No, no, no, you're not hearing me. This afternoon is too late. Send him now." He pauses, listening, before exploding again. "Don't tell me to calm down. YOU calm down."

"I know about engines," I tell the chubby guy. "My uncle's a mechanic. I'm here to help."

It's a white lie. It's exactly what Motti would have said.

"Seriously?"

I nod, giving him my best honest look. A couple of soldiers are leaning over the engine, arguing about which parts may or may not have broken.

"Come with me," he says. We skirt around the livid captain, who's still shouting into his radio.

My chubby soldier taps one of the other soldiers.

"What?" This one's young, with bushy, curly hair and thick sideburns.

"Show him the engine," my soldier tells him.

"Why? Who is this kid?"

"His uncle is a mechanic," the chubby soldier says. "This kid grew up around motors. He knows everything about engines."

I nod, going along with it.

The curly-haired solider hesitates, but after a moment, he shrugs as if to say, *Well, this day can't get any worse.*

"Here's the problem," the curly-haired soldier says to me. "The bus hit a bump in the road, and the engine just shut down and won't restart. It wasn't even a bad bump. We have eight hundred kilometers to go, and we broke down thirty minutes into the trip."

What he's not saying, because he thinks I don't know about the Egyptian prisoner exchange, is that with this delay, the whole swap is now in jeopardy. If we don't fix the bus and get it on the road soon, the Egyptians might suspect that Israel is playing some sort of trick. They might back out of the exchange altogether. They would never believe there was simply a breakdown on the side of the road.

My mouth goes dry. I want to help so badly, but what do I actually know about buses? Nothing.

"What's your name?" the chubby one asks me. He looks like someone who would normally be happy-go-lucky and quick to laugh. But right now, there are lines of stress and worry on his face.

"Beni," I say faintly.

"Beni, I'm Matan. That's Oren." He points to the curly-haired soldier.

"I really hope you can help us here," Matan says, gesturing at the massive engine.

When I first peer inside, my vision swims. This bus engine is totally different from a car engine. Everything is much bigger, and it's a diesel engine, which is built differently from a gas engine.

I shake my head. "I don't know this type of engine that well," I say weakly. My heart is racing. I feel horrible—guilty and ashamed. "Maybe I can't help with this."

"Come on," Matan says. "Your uncle is a mechanic. You're not even trying! Look, at least poke around. This is important."

The captain has ended his call.

"Who is this?" he demands. "What is going on here?"

Chapter Seventeen

It's a fair question.

Fifty Egyptian prisoners are on their way to Egypt. The transportation is broken, and peace in the Middle East is on the line. It's not exactly where you expect to find a twelve-year-old.

"I'm Beni," I say, as if that will clarify things.

"I don't believe this," the captain says, looking to the heavens. "I don't care what your name is," he says, looking back at me. "I don't know how you got here or who let you tinker with the bus"—here he glares at Matan, who visibly pales—"but you have exactly one minute to get out of here before I start arresting people."

"Captain!" Matan bursts out in a desperate rush. "This kid knows cars. He stopped to see if he can help with the bus."

The captain breathes heavily through his nose, his nostrils flared, as if straining for patience. "Are you a moron?" he asks Matan softly. Perhaps this is a rhetorical question. Matan doesn't answer. "This kid is ten. He's not a mechanic. I don't need another problem." The captain's voice rises as his temper erupts. "Get! Him! Away!"

Weirdly, being dismissed as useless, being ignored as the two soldiers argue, frees me to actually think about the problem in front of me. A bus that was working half an hour ago and is suddenly dead reminds me of Penina's car. Mickey rattled off several things that could cause that. I don't remember what they all were or how to fix them. But there is one thing I do know to look for, and at this point, I have nothing to lose by searching for it.

"I don't want to hear anything else from you," the captain screams, his face red and the tendons on either side of his neck bulging with rage. "Not one word! Get this ten-year-old out of here before I throw you in jail for disobeying orders."

Matan's shoulders slump in defeat, his face beet red with humiliation.

The captain, hands on hips, looks furious and helpless at the same time. Our eyes meet.

"Actually," I say to him, "I'm twelve."

"I don't care how old you are! Eight, ten, twelve, who cares? You need to get out of here."

"Can you give me a few more minutes?" I say. It's a huge engine, and I haven't had a chance to look at all of it.

Without waiting for his permission, I turn back and lean almost halfway into the engine block. There's something there. Something familiar. I just need a second. I reach, snaking my arm around the oil filter. I've almost got it.

"This is insane!" the captain shouts. "You're leaving now!"

Someone grabs me by the waistband of my shorts and pulls me away.

"Okay, okay," I say. The captain is huffing with fury, his hand on my shoulder. I pause. "But I know what's wrong with the bus."

Utter silence falls. The captain's hand clenches on my shoulder in surprise. I yelp and wiggle out of his grasp, rubbing the spot.

"Sorry," he apologizes. He takes a deep breath and releases it with a *whoosh*. "What's wrong with the bus?"

"Here," I say. I show him the bits of gray fur in my hand. "You've got mice. They chewed the cords. They must have been frayed when you pulled out, and then when the bus hit a bump or a pothole, they separated. That's why the engine died."

The two men stare at me with twin dumbfounded looks.

"Seriously?" the captain asks.

I nod. "Seriously. It's easy to fix."

The captain grins with relief. The sudden release of stress makes him look much younger. I realize he's only a few years older than Motti.

"If this works, I'm putting you in for a medal," he says. "You're a hero."

My face burns hot with the compliment, but I shrug off the praise. "I just need a pair of pliers, and if anyone has electrical tape—?"

The captain snaps his fingers, and two soldiers take off running to bring me the supplies I need.

I picture Mickey's hands as he stripped the plastic coating off the chewed wires in Penina's car and then spliced the exposed ends together. As soon as I have the pliers in my hand, I mimic those actions exactly as I remember, pulling back the coating to reveal the copper wires inside. Once both ends have their wires exposed, I twist them tightly. Someone hands me a strip of black electrical tape. I carefully wrap the tape around the new connection and step back.

"That should do it," I say. I'm excited and nervous. "See if it starts."

By now, news has spread that the bus is being repaired. A small crowd of soldiers has gathered around us. The tension makes the hot afternoon feel even more sweltering.

Will this work? My heart thumps, and my armpits are clammy. I use the back of my hand to wipe the sweat that beads on my forehead.

A soldier quickly hops into the bus and turns the key in the ignition. We all hold our breath, hoping for the same thing.

Will the bus start? Silence. There's a moment of petrified, frozen horror. Did I miss something?

I play it over in my mind: the spliced cords, twisted and wrapped in tape. Maybe I was wrong—

The engine comes to life with a roar.

Someone claps me on the back, and the blow is so unexpected that I nearly trip. Hands grab me, steadying me. Matan lifts me up, and the people around us cheer. I wave to what feels like a hundred people. Everyone is talking over one another. I grin ear-to-ear, feeling like the king of the world.

Someone who speaks Arabic hurries to tell the Egyptians they can board the bus. There's no time to waste, since the trip is already behind schedule. I'm lowered to the ground, and as I make my way over to the Egyptians, no one shouts at me to step back.

I take a breath to steady myself. This is the enemy. These men fight and kill Israelis. I want to see them before they return to Egypt. The next time I see an Egyptian might be when we're both in uniform, fighting each other in another war.

I stand by the bus door and watch as, one by one, the men climb in.

I don't know what I was expecting. Something menacing. Large men who glared threateningly. Wild eyes. Twitchy hands that itched to wrap around my neck.

I find myself shifting my weight to the balls of my feet, instinctively ready to run if one of them makes a grab for me.

The men get closer and closer.

My hands clench into fists. My heart knocks in my chest.

The first one walks by me. He spares me a quick look, curious as to what I'm doing here. But other than that, he's eager to board the bus.

My hands slowly unclench.

The second man passes me, close on the heels of the first. He looks worried. He keeps his eyes carefully on the ground as he boards, as if he's braced for someone to stop him. I suddenly realize that to him, *we're* the enemy. He's scared that we'll change our minds and he won't be allowed to return home.

One by one, the Egyptians walk by me. They don't look angry or hateful. In fact, other than their identical jumpsuits, they look no different from any Israeli I might pass on the street.

The next man who passes me smiles and nods in silent greeting.

He's probably in his mid-twenties, olive-skinned with curly dark hair. When he smiles, I catch sight of a big gap between his front teeth. He looks a lot like Yuval and Sara. They could almost be related.

I smile and nod back.

When all the Egyptians are in their seats, the driver closes the door.

I picture the long ride ahead for them, this bus rolling through the desert, past burned-out tanks and military vehicles half sunken in the shifting sands. I imagine it approaching the sparkling water of the Suez Canal, looking like a blue miracle cutting through the desert dunes. I picture the bus crossing the canal, driving into Egypt. I imagine the Egyptian passengers disembarking, meeting their families, hugging and kissing each other, crying with happiness and relief, going home.

I feel a rising joy in my chest.

Maybe everything will be fine after all.

Chapter Eighteen

"Are you sure you'll be okay getting back to the Golan?" Matan squints, looking at the empty road.

"It's no problem," I assure him. "I'll just flag down the next bus I see. Or hitchhike."

I've never done either of those things before, but in theory, one or the other should work. There's no way I want to delay the soldiers any further while we figure out a ride for me.

"All right then." Matan takes me at my word. "You've got food for the trip, right?"

I pat my full lunch pail.

"Well then." We shake hands. "Thank you."

"You did good today," the captain says.

A welcome breeze, heavy with sea salt and an ocean smell, cools the sweat on my temples and the back of my neck. I watch and wave as their armored jeep pulls onto the road and speeds up to catch up with the convoy heading south.

There's a tumble of feelings and thoughts rushing inside of me. The echoes of the cheers ring in my ears.

The Egyptians are going home—home to their parents, siblings, maybe wives and kids. I expected to see some mythical being: The Enemy. The one I'd heard so much about. But they're people. Ordinary people.

They're like Yuval. Like Motti. Like me. It's a strange thought.

A weird feeling of relief blooms. Somehow, seeing them safe and on their way home tells me Motti is safe and on his way home. I wonder if a twelve-year-old Egyptian kid is checking in on Motti.

I eat my lunch, a roll with sliced egg and tomato, as I wait for a bus. I would rather not hitchhike if I don't have to. By the time I finish eating, the sun has drifted noticeably lower in the sky, but no bus has driven by.

The Egyptians aren't the only ones on a tight

timeline. If I don't make it to Haifa before four, I won't be able to catch the last bus to Kibbutz Lavi. And then I'll be in big trouble. I don't have any money left, not even a phone token.

After a while, I realize I need to stick a thumb out and hope someone decides to stop.

The first driver who whizzes by doesn't even slow down to take a look. The next one toots the horn and waves, but I can see the car's packed front and back with boxes of produce. After that, there are no cars at all for a long time.

I'm really in trouble. I'm still hours away from home, and my parents will definitely beat me back. My heart sinks at the thought of how frantic my parents will feel.

Just when I'm starting to panic, I catch a glimpse of a familiar powder-blue car coming my way.

This is my chance. I jump up and down wildly, waving my arms to get the driver's attention. I succeed almost too well.

At the sight of me, she veers into the other lane and then overcompensates, yanking the wheel hard my way. She comes flying toward the shoulder, kicking up a plume of dust. I cough and blink specks of dirt out of my watery eyes as I hurry toward the car.

There are already a couple of soldiers in the passenger seats, and they have identical looks of bewildered surprise at the wild driving.

"Penina!" I cry out as I reach the car. The driver's-side window is rolled down. "I'm so glad to see you! It's Beni. Do you remember me?"

"You're Mickey's little helper, aren't you?" she says in surprise. "I'm just leaving my daughter and going back to Safed. What are you doing here?"

"The bus dropped me off here," I tell her, dodging the question. "Is there any way you can drive me to Kibbutz Lavi? It's not far from Safed."

"I picked up these folks so I could have some company on the long drive home," she says happily. "The more the better. Hop in."

The shorter, female soldier in the back scoots over and makes room.

As soon as I shut the door, Penina pulls away,

bumping over the curb and grinding the gears as she shifts. I see the two soldiers exchange glances, their eyes meeting in the crooked rearview mirror.

"It's okay," I tell them. "She drives like this all the time. We'll probably be fine."

"I survived two months in the Sinai," the guy in the front says. "I really don't want to die in a car wreck on my way home."

"You'll be fine," Penina says, patting his leg and swerving again. "I haven't killed anyone. Yet."

Fortunately, once we're really on our way, Penina's driving steadies. There are no lights or curbs to distract her anymore, only long straightaways past streams and farmland. We pass small towns and vast stretches of new forest. After a long, stressful day, I finally relax, sinking back into the fuzzy cloth seat in relief.

The soldier in the front seat looks like he's in his mid-twenties, about the same age Gideon would have been. It's easy to imagine Gideon in his army uniform, hitching a ride home. As if he can feel my gaze, the soldier swivels in his seat, looking back at me.

"Where are you coming from?" I ask, just to make conversation.

"I've been at Kilometer 101 for the past month," he says with a sigh.

"You've come from Egypt?" I ask. "My brother's there right now. He's a prisoner."

"Oh no!" Penina exclaims in shock. "That's terrible."

The soldier next to me looks at me with concern. "I'm so sorry to hear it," she says, touching my arm.

"He'll be released soon," I say. "The exchange is starting today."

"God willing," Penina says.

The soldier in the front seat sighs again. "This awful war. It's been even worse than the War of Attrition or the Six-Day War."

"Did you fight during the Six-Day War?" the soldier next to me asks him. She looks younger than him, so she probably wasn't involved with that conflict.

"In Jerusalem," he says. "I was there when the Old City was unified."

"My oldest brother was in Jerusalem then

too," I say. "But he didn't live to see the city reunified."

The soldier tilts his head and squints a little as he stares at me. "Who was your brother?" he asks.

"Gideon," I say. I suddenly realize how rarely I speak my brother's name out loud. So I say it again. "His name was Gideon Laor."

The soldier draws in a breath sharply. Goose-bumps cover my arms.

"I knew Gideon," says the soldier.

Everyone gasps in surprise at the coincidence.

I lock eyes with him. It feels like a miracle. Here is someone who knew Gideon, who has different memories and stories about him. I didn't think I would ever hear new stories about my brother.

"I can see it. You look so much like him," the soldier says in wonder. "I'm Boaz, by the way."

"Beni," I tell him.

"Beni," Boaz says, "Gideon saved my life. We were going hard against the Jordanians. I was eighteen years old, people were screaming, it was dark. I couldn't tell what was going on. I was standing there like an idiot, and Gideon came out of nowhere, like Superman. He grabbed me and pulled me into a ditch, right as shots were fired exactly where I'd been standing."

Everyone in the car is quiet for a moment.

"We got separated on the second day of the war. I never saw him again. But I still think about him."

"I do too," I say quietly.

Boaz sits in silence briefly before he swivels back around to face me. "I can't quite believe this. Gideon has been on my mind so much lately." He reaches for my hand and squeezes it. "It's really great to meet you."

My heart aches yet pulses with happiness at the same time. "Thank you," I croak. I clear my throat. "Thank you for telling me that."

I would rather have Gideon alive and here, but since that isn't possible, I can't imagine anything better than meeting someone who knew him and learning that Gideon lives on in his memory.

"May his memory be a blessing," Penina says, summing up my thoughts perfectly. It's the traditional thing to say about someone who's died, but I've never realized how true that wish could be. "This is *bashert*," she goes on. "This is fate bringing you two together. It has to be." She sniffles loudly. "I can't wait until I tell my daughter."

She reaches for a tissue, and the car veers toward the shoulder.

"Watch out!" we all scream, and Penina quickly straightens the car.

"Sorry," she says lightly.

"If you or your parents ever want to talk about Gideon, I'd be happy to meet with you," Boaz says. "If we survive this car ride," he adds under his breath. He scribbles his contact information on a piece of paper and hands it to me. I carefully fold it and tuck it into my pocket.

Penina launches into a story about someone she once knew who bumped into someone they knew in the middle of a monsoon in India, but I quickly lose track of the twists and turns of the story. She talks the whole way, but while she's talking, her eyes stay on the road, which is better for all of us.

Eventually, the soldier next to me closes her eyes. Boaz keeps nodding off to sleep, his head jerking up as it starts falling forward. There's a peaceful feeling in the car. I rest my head against the window.

I wake up when the car comes to a stop.

"All right, my young friend," Penina says, reaching back and tapping me on the knee. "First stop, Kibbutz Lavi! Hurry home now. It's late."

I rub my eyes and wipe a slick of drool that's pooled by my cheek.

"Take care of yourself and your parents," Boaz says.

"Thanks, Boaz," I say, opening the door. The cold, late afternoon air of the Golan washes in, instantly waking me. "And thanks for the ride, Penina."

"Anytime, doll," she says.

Soon afterward, the last local bus of the evening arrives. I still have an hour to go before I'm home, but I can beat my parents there.

The ride is uneventful. When the bus reaches my stop, I expect the moshav to be quiet, settling in for the night. I figure there won't be anyone at the bus stop in front of the main gates. But to my surprise, I see Sara, Ori, and Yoni sitting on the ground, tossing small pebbles up in the air and catching them again. They scramble to their feet as I disembark.

"What are you guys doing here?" I ask in disbelief.

The bus pulls away, engulfing us in a cloud of exhaust.

"We've been waiting for you, dummy," Sara says. She waves her hand in front of her face to scatter the fumes.

"What? All day?" I ask.

"Pretty much," Yoni says. "Since school let out."

For a moment, I'm struck speechless. "Why?" I finally ask. "Why would you do that?"

"We had to make sure you got home okay," Sara says. She blinks behind her thick-rimmed glasses. "Another hour and we were going to have to tell our parents."

A warm glow starts forming in my chest. My friends. My friends were worried about me.

"I wanted to catch the next bus and go after you," she adds.

"But I talked her out of it," Ori says. "There was no way we could catch you, and it would slow you down if all of us tried to make it into the base."

"We figured the next-best thing was to wait for you here," Yoni concludes. "So did you? Did you see the Egyptians?"

The three of them look at me expectantly.

"Yeah," I say. "I did."

We all fall silent for a moment. A gust of cold wind blows, hinting at the winter storms to come.

"And?" Ori asks with a shiver. "What did you think?"

I'm not sure how to explain that they looked sad and scared and hopeful. That each of them has two eyes, a nose, and a mouth, like we do. That some were handsome and some were not. That they have families back home who are really worried for them.

"We're going to have peace with them," I say out loud. The glowing red taillights of the bus disappear around the bend. We're illuminated by a single light from the lamp post, shining down over us.

"You think?" Sara asks. She sounds hopeful and cautious.

"Yeah," I say, almost in a daze. I smile. "We're so much alike. We'll find a way to work it out."

Chapter Nineteen

It's 7 p.m. and already dark. It isn't safe for Sara to walk back to her moshav alone.

"My mom can give you a ride," Yoni offers. The four of us walk to his house together.

As soon as we open his front door, Dor comes running out to meet us. He's grown taller since I last saw him two months ago.

"Be-ni," he says when he sees me. "Be-ni!" He's got food stains on his white shirt, and his hair is rumpled with sweat and traces of tomato sauce. He grins at me, flashing tiny white teeth.

"Hi, Dor," I say, sinking down so we're eye to eye. I tickle his tummy.

He giggles and squirms away. His eyes are bright and twinkly. I can't help but grin back.

He's happy and healthy. He really is okay.

"We talk about you all the time," Dor's mom says, watching us with a fond eye. "We tell him how you saved him. You're his hero. I've been hoping you'd stop by and see him."

I blink in shock. I can hardly believe I'm hearing this. After all the guilt and sleepless nights I went through, they think I'm a hero? "I thought you might be mad at me," I say sheepishly.

"Are you crazy?" she asks.

"What's wrong with you?" Yoni demands. He smacks me on the back of my head.

"Ouch!" I cry.

"Don't do that to your friend," Ronit scolds Yoni.

Yoni tells his mom that Sara needs a ride to her moshav.

"No problem, Sara," she says. "You boys just need to stay and watch the little ones until I'm back."

"My dad is at Nafah," Yoni explains. I won't lie: I'm relieved when he says that.

While Ronit drives Sara to her moshav,

Yoni, Ori, and I stay to watch Dor and Shoshi. We hang out, teasing and cracking jokes. At some point, Dor ends up on my lap. He rests his head on my shoulder. As Ori and Yoni exclaim in disgust over Shoshi's full diaper, the toddler's warm weight grows heavier on my chest. By the time Yoni finishes cleaning the baby, Dor has fallen asleep in my arms. For the first time since we moved here from Jerusalem, I feel relaxed.

"Yoni," I say, after hesitating for a moment, "is your dad mean to you a lot?"

Ori freezes and then looks away.

Yoni's ears turn red. There's that familiar look on his face, the one that's so much like his dad's. I wonder if he wants to hit me again. But after making my way alone to Atlit and back, saving the prisoner exchange, and meeting someone who knew Gideon, I'm not scared.

"I just want to know if you're okay," I say.

Yoni takes a deep breath and lets it out slowly. The sudden tension in the room eases.

"He's really changed since Dor got hurt. I think it made him realize what's really important, you know?"

His thoughtful look of hope warms me.

When Yoni's mom returns, she carefully scoops Dor out of my arms. She kisses his sleepy head and takes him to the room he shares with Yoni. It's time for me to head home.

"See you tomorrow," Yoni says.

"Yeah," Ori says. He punches me lightly on the shoulder. "No skipping school tomorrow, okay?"

"Okay," I say, smiling sheepishly. "I'll be there."

* * *

After all that, I beat my parents home. It's past eight, and I start to wonder if I should be worried about them. I'm reading a novel on the couch in the living room when they walk in. I can instantly tell something is different about them. There's a look on their faces, a charge of energy in the air.

It turns out I wasn't the only one with a secret agenda today.

"Beni," my mom says, "look who's here."

She steps to the side to reveal the person behind her, standing next to my dad.

I have no memory of rising from the couch, the book falling to the floor.

I have no memory of screaming with joy.

I have no memory of running, flat-out running, toward him.

I have no memory of launching myself into the air.

I only remember this: Motti walking in through our front door.

The next thing I know, I'm hugging him so tightly and he's hugging me back so hard that I can barely breathe.

"Motti," I say. "Motti. You're back."

He's wearing his uniform, but it smells different. With a jolt, I realize this must be what Egyptian laundry soap smells like. It's not a bad smell, just different from what I'm used to. The Egyptians who went home today will smell like us, like Israeli laundry soap.

"Beni," he says. He kisses my ear. "How are you? Are you okay?"

"You're asking me if *I'm* okay? Of course I'm

okay. You're here. How could I not be okay?"

My parents watch us, my mom wiping tears of happiness.

"Do you like our surprise?" my dad asks.

"There was never a counselor?" I ask.

"There was; we met with her first," my mom says.

"We didn't want to get your hopes up, since we didn't know which flight Motti would be sent home on," my dad explains. "We met with the counselor, and then we went to the airport without telling you."

I shake my head in amazement.

"And there's this," I say. It's time to give my parents and Motti the best present I can possibly think of. I pull out a crumpled piece of paper with Boaz's number. "I met someone who knew Gideon. He has the most amazing story to tell you."

My mother clasps her hands and presses them to her chest. "Oh, my goodness, how in the world did you meet him? Or figure out that he knew Gideon?" she asks.

"Uh, it's a long story," I say.

My dad takes the slip of paper and carefully smooths it like I've handed him a precious treasure map.

Motti is thinner, and he looks tired, but he smiles and ruffles my hair like he knows I've been up to something.

My stomach gives a loud growl. I haven't eaten dinner.

"Are you hungry, my boys?" My mom smiles. That spark of hers is back, and I have no doubt that the food she's about to prepare will taste great. "Motti, we have all your favorite things."

Motti grins. It isn't quite as lighthearted or broad as his old smile, but I'll take it. "A cheese omelet with salad sounds amazing right now."

It does. My stomach gurgles in happy anticipation.

"Coming right up!"

We all follow her into the kitchen. With the cheerful smell of cooking and the bright light, we take our usual seats around the table. Finally, it all feels right. Everyone in their seats, the table balanced by the four of us.

We dig into the food my mom lays out. The hot, cheesy omelets. The crisp, lemony salad. The crusty rolls that scatter sesame seeds as we rip them to dip into smears of hummus.

In a few hours, a few hundred miles to the south, hundreds of Egyptians will arrive home, maybe even to eat the same food: hummus, salad, rolls—the food of the Middle East. Maybe they're thinking that they smell like Israeli laundry soap and that it doesn't smell bad. Maybe they're thinking they've met Israelis and that we look a lot like them. Maybe they're thinking, like me, that it's possible to stop hating, to stop fighting.

I swallow a mouthful of food. The feeling of happiness and hope fills me to the brim. Our *maybe* has been answered. Our Motti is back. Maybe there are more happy *maybes* in our future.

Maybe.

It's not such a bad word after all.

Afterword

The Yom Kippur War was a traumatic war for Israelis. The Egyptians and Syrians, who six years earlier had been quickly defeated in the Six-Day War, completely surprised Israel with their 1973 attack on Yom Kippur. During the first week of the war, the Israeli military, which had been considered nearly unbeatable, suffered huge losses and stunning setbacks, the full extent of which were not clear until much later.

Though the tide of the war turned after the first week and a lot of lost ground was recovered, the experience forever shattered Israelis' illusions about the invincibility of their military, intelligence gathering, and government.

However, something interesting happened in the aftermath of the Yom Kippur War. Whereas the lopsided victory of the Six-Day War left the region seething with mutual mistrust and disdain, the hard-fought draw of the Yom Kippur War allowed Egypt and Israel to—if not trust or like each other—at least acknowledge a mutual respect. That respect helped pave the way for a peace treaty between the two countries six years later.

Signed on March 26, 1979, the treaty brought peace between Egypt and Israel for the first time since Israel's creation in 1948, as well as a Nobel Peace Prize to the Egyptian president, Anwar Sadat, and the Israeli prime minister, Menachem Begin.

That peace has lasted to this day.

Acknowledgments

My father was an Israeli officer who saw active duty during the Yom Kippur War. He was a newlywed when the war broke out, and when he kissed my mother goodbye to report for duty, they expected to see each other again in a week. It was six months before they were reunited. One night while he was stationed across the Suez Canal with no way to communicate with his family back in Israel, he heard the radio message that my mother had sent him: *Hello Gaby, from your wife, Liora, who loves you.* It meant the world to him to hear those personal words from his beloved while he was so far away. I knew I had to include that detail when I wrote this book. Sharp readers might remember that Beni overhears that message as he plays chess with his grandfather.

Before I could write this book, I traveled to Israel so that I could visit the Golan Heights and walk through the fields where the tank battles raged. While there, I was lucky enough to speak to many Israelis who took time from their busy lives to tell me about their experiences during the Yom Kippur War. My profound thanks to Retired General Meir Elran, Yehuda Harel, Varda Hershkowitz, Dr. Ephraim Kam, Yacob Kochav, Rafi Kornfeld, Sara Kornfeld, Gabriel Laufer, Liora Laufer, Deena Moses, Zvi Moses, Mickey Obed, Retired General Giora Romm, Yardena Rosen, Zvika Rosen, Bezalel Rubin, Ronith Shemer, and Esther Yehezkel.

Lynne Sandler generously shared a copy of the diary she kept while living in Israel during the Yom Kippur War. Luckily for me, she has a writer's eye for detail. There really was a screening of *The Emperor's New Clothes* on television the day after Yom Kippur, a change in the regular programming to keep children distracted and entertained. That and many other aspects of her daily life as noted in her diary helped enrich this book with authentic specifics.

I read many books and newspaper articles to help me understand the Yom Kippur War. Several that particularly illuminated the time period for me were *Lioness: Golda Meir and the Nation of Israel* by Francine Klagsbrun, *Israel: A Concise History of a Nation Reborn* by Daniel Gordis, *Solitary: The Crash, Captivity and Comeback of an Ace Fighter Pilot* by Giora Romm, and *The Yom Kippur War: The Epic Encounter That Transformed the Middle East* by Abraham Rabinovich.

I owe a huge debt of gratitude to the phenomenal people at PJ Library, Sifriyat Pijama, PJ Our Way, and the Harold Grinspoon Foundation, who in general have done so much to support Jewish literature for children and in particular helped support my research and writing. A special thanks to Catriella Freedman, Neta Shapira, and Galina Vromen.

My critique group—Pamela Ehrenberg, Caroline Hickey, Kristin Levin, and Erica Perl (title maven!)—read early drafts of this manuscript, and their insightful editing and support helped sustain me through multiple drafts and rewrites. Madelyn Rosenberg read a late version of the manuscript under a tight deadline (my hero!), and her suggestions helped me with the final push. My editor, Amy Fitzgerald, was delightful to work with, and her discerning edits made the book shine. My dear longtime agent, Stephen Barbara, finds my stories their homes and rolls with all the ideas and changes and what-ifs that I throw at him; thank you for believing in my work. (As a note to those of you curious about the writing process: I have seven folders with very different versions of this story. Writing a book takes patience and stamina.)

Finally, a huge thank you, hug, and kiss to my family. Fred, my first reader, my sounding board, my best friend, thank you for always believing I should write—and for being the kind, patient, wise man you are. Tovar, thank you for the terrific suggestions you've made to help make this book and others so much better. Delaney, thank you for being a bright spark of creativity and insight. I love you all so much. You make everything brighter.

Sweet Lime Photography

About the Author

Tammar Stein is the author of novels for teens and children. Her books include *Light Years*, an American Libraries Association Best Book of the Year and a Virginia Reader's Choice, and *The Six-Day Hero*, a Sydney Taylor Honor book, a Junior Library Guild Selection, and a prequel to *Beni's War*. Tammar lives in Singapore with her family and rambunctious hound dog.